Soothing Ironies

Ana Grasya

Ukiyoto Publishing

All global publishing rights are held by

Ukiyoto Publishing

Published in 2023

Content Copyright © Ana Grasya

ISBN 9789360160708

All rights reserved.
No part of this publication may be reproduced, transmitted, or stored in a retrieval system, in any form by any means, electronic, mechanical, photocopying, recording or otherwise, without the prior permission of the publisher.

The moral rights of the author have been asserted.

This is a work of fiction. Names, characters, businesses, places, events, locales, and incidents are either the products of the author's imagination or used in a fictitious manner. Any resemblance to actual persons, living or dead, or actual events is purely coincidental.

This book is sold subject to the condition that it shall not by way of trade or otherwise, be lent, resold, hired out or otherwise circulated, without the publisher's prior consent, in any form of binding or cover other than that in which it is published.

www.ukiyoto.com

*For those whose minds
make a beautiful catastrophe.*

Introduction

Here are some scattered snippets from a heart so restless that it tends to sway with the hand of creativity, teasing rhymes to dance with ink at two in the morning. *Soothing Ironies* is an anthology of the beautiful catastrophes I birthed after arranging the pieces from my first book, *Bygones*. While Bygones contains chapters gravitating to a particular tone engulfing the reader into a riveting shift of emotions, this book presents prose and poetry unapologetically spilled all over the pages without following a certain theme. You can read chronologically or in reverse, from any page you prefer. You can skim off the middle; this book is free and unconventional. It was not designed to follow a certain storyline. Yet if you bury your nose between the lines, you will discover that somehow, each piece was given an integrity to shriek out its own *soothing ironies*.

Ironies. There are some forces in the universe that cannot be tamed. *Time, love, death,* each assumes a quality that is difficult to conquer.

You cannot befriend time. It waits for no man.

You cannot cage love. It flies across the blue sky.

You cannot escape death. It will fetch you anyhow.

Time. Some would say time is just an *illusion*. It's not real. Humans invented it to somehow simplify the complexity of our origin. In the beginning, there wasn't really time. Just a void gaping. Then men, in pursuit of measuring accumulated moments created a scale that divided the vast spaces into *time*. Time. Now it became so real that we tend to chase it, befriend it. The irony is that, time *has no master.* It doesn't wait for anyone. Thus, we break when we lose it. But then again, we don't seem to realize its value until it's gone.

Love. It's our universal language. It binds us, divides us. We all want it. *"A million times more crimes were committed in the name of love than in the name of hate."* It is enough to make us forget ourselves. It is enough to transform just anyone regardless of status, and race, and culture. We become so enslaved with the idea of it. Who wouldn't want to soar into the seventh heaven? Some try to cage it. The thing about love however is that, it ought to be free. It doesn't deserve to be imprisoned. It's a swift and fleeting emotion. Something we could only crave for once. For that one time is forever. And just like time, we only realize its worth *when it's gone.*

Death. This is something everyone fears. We are all afraid to die. We all loath ending. Nevertheless, this is a part of the cycle. It's something we cannot escape. *It's a destiny.* Just like the books we read, we will all become stories. We all need to die so others can be born. And what will become of the moments we accumulated in our own expanse? These will feed the next generation's hungry hearts. They will talk about us in the next one hundred years. We will become the lessons. We will become the heroes. Some will be inked in history. Some will remain unsung. It's ironic though that because of fear, we never really live while we're alive. Thus, the regrets whispered in deathbeds.

Time.

Love.

Death.

All of these, as explicated emanate *ironies*. Ironies that are keen, they cut so deep. Yet somehow, the blood that gushes out from the wound these ironies cause becomes the hand that moves the pen. The pen glides against the crisp paper, creating a rustle as it stains stories each wound dictates. While words spill out, the heart where the irony runs deep is comforted. The words soothe where it burns the most as the ironies play with the cursive being tainted, reliving moments that are long forgotten, recollecting emotions concealed within the burrows of time. I hope as your eyes sweep against each page, you will recollect your own ironies and soothe yourself with the truth that you're not alone in the bitterness. You're not alone in the pangs. You're not alone in the progression of your suffering.

We mirror each other's suffering. We find our own hearts in books, in magazines, in a piece of paper crumpled and thrown at the corner of the street. Sometimes the words that we wish we could say are found in a stranger's art, in somebody's journal. As I write, I wish I would be able to breathe life to a stranger's silent screams, to a neighbor's whispered prayers, to a friend's austere wishes. As I write, I wish I can represent some of your ironies and soothe you with the truth that emotions—may they be dampening or uplifting, are relative. I feel what you feel; you feel what I feel, perhaps in different degree but the truth stays. We mirror each other's love stories, bitterness, fears, frustrations and the like.

I ardently wish I can soothe your ironies anyhow.

Love,

Ana Grasya

If I pass away,
my pen will mourn me longer
than my friends will ever do
in a lifetime
It will sit cold on my study table,
its own bereavement festers
with the lifeless body buried
somewhere, reeking of lost
poetry,
an ocean of mystery that seems
unsolvable now that the lead
vanished like smoke
It will try to recollect the words
it used to scribble
and the emotions they carry
It will marvel at the depth of the scars
that resonate on the seemingly
flawless pieces
How many times in a day did I survive
the pangs before I decided the
culmination of a barren life?
Such a tragedy that it could only
lie there, thinking of the past as
its yearning to be held burns
with a candlestick

-*mourn me longer*

We won't
make it out *alive*
though we work
so hard to keep the fire,
the embers burning
warming our hands
melting the ice
hugging our hearts
We won't
make it out *breathing*
The ultimate destiny is *death*
though we keep denying
its entry,
always leaving it cold,
shuddering
from the afternoon breeze,
it looms,
waits for us to succumb,
sits with the audience,
anticipates
our final bow

-ultimate destiny

Stories crawling
out of a bludgeoned heart
bleeding, burning
under the scorching sun
The words wash
against unknown banks,
ripples of water
licking the rim of a basin
that contained journeys inked—
proof of existence rustling
against crisp paper neatly piled
on a wordsmith's desk
I wait
for the clumsy scribbles,
letters gushing
from a well-trained quill
I'll savor
all of the tales tumbling
from a dead man's lips
who reckoned love
tastes better
from a devil's tongue

-wordsmith's desk

But what advantage
do I have over her?
A face resembling
Mona Lisa
An exquisite art,
she belongs
to the Louvre
my love,
while *I*—
I belong with
the heavy hearts peopling
the lonely streets holding
easels and a dream
they try to burn
with a stick
of cigarette!

*(I pray
that you'll choose me
anyhow.)*

- *an easel and a dream*

I've slain dreams
and now they fill
the empty space stretching
as far as the eyes can reach
Beyond the Maginot Line,
I buried them without putting
an epitaph
Now they haunt
my sleeping heart,
knocking, trying
to stir the warmth
that enveloped
my freezing fragments
I may be guilty
but so is *society*
So, I'm dragging it
along with the faceless monsters
whose machinations crippled
dreams, pushing them
into the grave with me!

-beyond the maginot line

Maybe I loved you immediately after we talked for the first time. Maybe I fell too hard like a meteorite but tried to silence the screams of the heart I thought was dead. *I don't know.* If you ask me when exactly did I fall in love with you, I have no answer. *It just happened.* Maybe love is supposed to come like a thief in the middle of the night, take your heart and sanity away while you're sleeping.

Maybe I fell in love with you that rainy afternoon we shared an umbrella that could barely cover us so we ended up completely drenched. It can also be during that Thursday night when we stopped at *8th Avenue Coffee* after enduring a boring lecture. I remember how we started talking about everything while missing the whole point of casting each other gazes that were more intent than necessary. You talked about your lost love and all the reasons why people have to leave. You told me of the essence of forgiveness and letting go. I wrote you a poem that night—each line, a poignant expression of everything I was dying to say to you in person but refuse to materialize in my breath when we talk. I promised myself the piece of inked emotions will reach your door somehow. It reached your inbox at dawn. Maybe it was when you called me to say how much you loved it that I let my caged heart fly in frenzy. *I am not quite sure.*

It can also be when you declared we're going to be the *"weird friends"* at school that my sleeping heart stirred for the first time in a hundred years. Or that night when we took the luxury of time to explore the city in your motorcycle in the midst of cold drizzles. You told me it was the craziest thing you ever did in your life. We stopped at McDonald's for fries and a deadly dose of coffee. Maybe it was when you said if I were a religion, you would convert right away that the fortress I built around me began to crack. I wish I know exactly when I started losing my head over you. *But I don't.*

So, I play with the double-edged sword that is *maybe*.

Maybe—a word for a room of possibilities, none of which could expunge the myriads of regret that are now hammering inside my head. Maybe I took it too far. I had you in arm's length. If I just told you I love you right *then* and *there* instead of trying to determine the exact time when I caught this love bug, you could've been mine. However, my love, I concerned myself too much with time that I failed to notice you're drifting away from me.

So maybe I lost you because I was too particular with time.

Or maybe not.

-*time, love, and countless maybes*

How can you call it *love*
when all I can see
are *scars*
carved all over
      a
          once
                flawless
                        skin?

- ***scars all over***

I bought a one-way ticket
to the other side
of the moon
Watch the ocean rise
as I fall
asleep in the arms
of darkness
A friend returning
from a short voyage,
he cradles my head,
traces the cracked skull
with his fingers
until I sigh
with the thunder clapping
over my weeping sky!

-one way ticket

Vibrant hues painting
the afternoon skies
Fiery red and orange
reminding me of your last goodbye
and the truth
that the tears
have been dried for a while
Puff of zephyr
kissing my eyes, whispering
words that make me smile
Oh darling,
who would have known
the pains
you buried so deep
within me
left me bolder
and wiser
and more observant
of the evanescent
truth about the sunset:
Sometimes splendid
things happen
after every goodbye!

-evanescent

Still, I wait for you
for I am your ever faithful,
deeply besotted lover
gripping the thin chance
that ties
your heart to my fingertips
You've gone away
too soon, I failed to say
how much you mean
and so, *I'll wait*
Though the distance paved
between us grows
unbridgeable,
I'll stay
where you left me
watching the clouds
condense,
ready to precipitate
with my abundant tears!

- *the clouds condense*

It's *ironic* how I love you so much while you can't even recognize me from the sea of faces. You didn't hear my call, passed me by without glancing at all. Yet *I am glad.* Everyone admires you.

You're my ***Haley's comet.***

And me? I am the shooting star who fell to make your dream come true. While it's painful to fall and end up unrecognized by your heart, I am willing to do it a thousandfold in the name of *love*.

I'll just behold you from afar.

-haley's comet

My heart died that day. I didn't know hearts could actually die until I started feeling mine slip away into another dimension; *somewhere cold, somewhere dark, somewhere there's no you.* All our memories tumbled down like tears rolling themselves into oblivion. The long conversations finally reached a *dead end*; turned themselves around and started marching back to the lips that breathed life to them.

I felt it all. How our eyes stopped exchanging warm gazes. How we suddenly shunned each other's call. How love departed from my system like a soul leaving its earthly form. Not that all of these matter now that I have turned dark and cold. But there are certain points in time and space, some worthy coordinates that remind me of everything. Sometimes it all comes back to me—the *love*, the *you*, the *time* we left behind.

I am sorry I have to die that way. That I have to choose freedom over you. That I have to choose power over you. Everything is a concept. The euphoria, the maddening twists of emotions—*all of these are concepts,* none of which are lasting. So, I let my heart wither away like a plant. You held it tight before it died, squeezed it so hard that all your claw marks were etched on it—a beautiful proof that in spite of yourself, you never really wanted to let go.

I am looking at these marks now as I ponder on the daunting serenity of this new dimension where I loiter like a lost soul. They say *love doesn't exist*. I've been told so many times that there's no such thing in nature. But while I create new memories with myself, waves of emotions so strong come back to me. Like ropes, they bind me to the *you* I try so hard to forget. I am always trapped between the pangs of forgetting and remembering. My mind, no matter how I confine it within my control, it always wanders back to where I came from—to the place where I left all the memories of you.

Sometimes I want to come back. However, my love, I cannot. For the heart that gave life to my universe died that day. That day when you were too proud to look me in the eye and say *it's over*. Well, you didn't really have to. I felt it when you leaned to kiss me for the last time. Your lips, oh love your lips were nothing but a cold and dead flesh touching my slowly desolating soul.

-back to where I came from

She asks love where he's been
She's been waiting ever since
Sitting under the moonlight,
she watches shadows dance
and cascade before her eyes
He smiles so gently,
touches her trembling lips
"I've always been here", says he,
"Waiting for you to seek me!"

-always been here

When you gaze,
the skin that covers me detaches
itself
like a silk
        f
          a
            l
              l
                i
                  n
                    g

                        off,
                        revealing
                        my throbbing
                        fury,
                        my secret longings,
                        my *sins*...

-detachment

He stood in the doorway
a phantom eyeing me
Crumpled papers in his arms,
dried ink stained his heart
I can't repress the shudder
that abruptly rose within me
as he paced the line that parted
his ghostly self from me
He handed me the paper
where he wrote all his dreams
 I read each word in tears
every verse spoke of me
I gazed at his bloodshot eyes
they twinkled back at me
I rose to plant a kiss,
he trembled against my lips
Now I can claim it's true
what people always say
"When a writer loved you so,
you can never die!"

- ***dried ink and crumpled paper***

I'm the girl
who stitched
the stars
at the hem
of her skirt
because
it gives her joy
watching them
twinkle
as she turns
round and round
until totally collapsing
to the ground

-stitch the stars

To the person who came too late,

Believe me, it will all make sense one day. So, lift your spirit up and trust that somewhere, there's a *"beautiful reason"* why we can't be together, why we should not be together. And that beautiful reason is someone the whole universe handpicked to be *your perfect match*. When you meet her, I hope you will think of me. When she takes your hand, I hope you will remember to smile and more importantly, this night. This night when you sulk over the bitterness of rejection while I patiently remind you of your worth. When she gazes at your eyes, I hope you will take a minute to thank the night sky, the stars, the whole universe for helping you find what you have been looking for. When she kisses your lips, I hope you can finally be happy. And in that moment of celebration, I hope you will remember to whisper these words to the wind, praying they will reach me, wherever I may be, *"Tama ka!* (You're right!)

Let's pour ourselves
some drinks
not because it's Friday
but because drinks
remind me
of how you crawled
under my skin,
allowing me
to breathe
into your nostrils
and feel how the life
was *slowly*,
painfully
siphoned from you
The weight
you carried
on your shoulders,
all the insults,
the accusations—
oh, how they pierced you
until you're a total wreck

Now you're gone

You're gone
but I can still taste you
from this glass
The lips that taught me
how to love,
I remember them
as my soul mourns

all the chances
I got to say
I love you
but didn't…

I didn't
I chose to cling
to my pride—
the same damn pride
that haunts me
every time
I remember you

And I can only cry,
bleed for a while
for what good is being alive,
if the heart
that made me survive
all my frights
is now buried
six feet
underground?

-*fridays and regrets*

You're looking at dead stars!
Don't stare deeper,
tear your eyes away
for mine have long been
dead,
you won't see a twinkle,
just hydrogen running out
The life that kept them burning
eloped with the night
while I was waiting
darling,

and you came too late

- ***dead stars***

I never felt lonely when I'm alone but since I met you, I get lonely when surrounded by people. My eyes seek you among the hostile faces. Of course, you aren't there.

I miss you.

The aroma of coffee filling my room smells like your perfume. Its blackness that stares at me like a void drawing my soul to the unknown reminds me of how I am nothing without you.

I miss you.

When I walk in my bare feet in the middle of the night, the coldness of the tiled floor touching my skin makes me think of dead conversations—those deep talks that stopped all of a sudden, leaving me lost in the endless corridor of time. I linger in that moment when warmth enveloped me like loving arms. I never thought one day, coldness would crawl into my skin as I stare at the empty space you once occupied beside me.

I miss you

The smell coming from the pages of my new book makes my mind wander back to the time when you told me you can read minds. Mine, however baffled you like a math problem you just can't figure out. So, I held your hand, that simple touch revealed everything I ever kept inside. And you understood. *Or did you?* I am not certain of that now. Because if you really did, why aren't you here?

I miss you.

Even the streets are empty. The pedestrians look like ghosts mumbling to each other unintelligible phrases which for me, are *dead*—dead like everything I ever wrote, like those *haikus* I managed to scribble in class while pretending to absorb the lecture. I tried to immortalize you in a three-line poem containing 5-7-5 *moras*. But those lines which talked about how close we were to falling in love are now the guns firing deadly shots at me. I guess I am deader than all the empty phrases I hear from strangers because you, the life that once filled me with light, are gone.

I miss you.

After you slammed the door, shut me out like a pariah, I've been questioning if I've ever been good enough for anyone. I am always less perhaps because I am an unfixable mess. It hurts that even you, of all people, left me hanging. Of all the things you could have done, you chose to *break me*. But...

I miss you.

And I hate that I keep missing you. Even after you turned your back from me, my entire being clings to you and all the promises you ever made. I know those words don't mean a thing but I'm holding them like sweet salvation. It's pathetic. I wish there was a *statute of limitation* to missing someone who doesn't even care to cast a glance—one last glance to check if I broke in perfect symmetry.

I miss you.

How could I not? You are the coffee stains spilled all over my notes, the bubble of thoughts that just keep popping up even if I don't want to. You are the stars that I try to count when sleep seems to be a slipping reality, the books that I read, the bedtime stories, the songs. *The songs.* This is even more wounding than the former mentions. Despite of everything you did, you are still the voice I want to hear singing my favorite song, while I fall for you all over again, like I've never been a ramshackle after losing you.

I miss you

Sometimes I stay awake
to dream of you
for a while

-awake to dream

I catch the first drop of rain on my palm and think about how long you have waited for it. You told me you wish to fall in love before the first rain of November. It's been raining for weeks now, my love, and every drop reminds me of the reasons why you had to wait for this season. Though I exhaust my wit trying to get the wisdom behind it, I don't understand. *I can't understand.*

Why did you wait? Why did the rain come too late? Too late for you to feel it glide on your face. Too late for you to catch it on your palm. Sometimes I try to question Cupid. Why *you?* Why *me?* Why in the universe did we wait? If he has a conscience, why did he allow us to wait this long? Now you're gone and the sky just won't stop raining.

I still don't get it. My world will be flooded soon and I will still be here trying to unravel the wisdom behind the course of waiting you chose to tread when you could have just fallen in love with me. I wish I could have just ignored your *"first rain fantasy"* and fell in love with you while I had the chance.

- ***waited for the rain to fall***

It's silly
> B
> U
> T
> it feels like we only wake up so we won't
break the hearts of the ones we love.

-won't break the hearts

Tick, tack, tick tack, it's eleven thirty on the clock
Tick tack, tick tack, pain is dripping into my blood
I make a move to prevent the piercing wave
Yet with my flesh quavering, the piercing ache came

I always thought I was brave and strong
Would be fine alone or immersed in throng
But why do I keep singing all our song
Like I'd never forget you all along?

Tick, tack, tick tack this heart starts to crumble
In drunkenness, I sway and then I stumble
Thorns cut into my flesh I started bleeding
As I call you—oh, it's your love I'm heeding!

Yet even your shadow seems elusive
Your eyes oh, how they prefer to be evasive
Listen to the cadence of my agonized cry
If I have to reach for you from afar, I'll try

Cause it's eleven thirty and I'm soaked
So drenched in a quagmire of desolation
And I break down, frail hands waving for hope
Come redeem me before I fall to destruction

I quaver, I bleed—the clock keeps going
Reach out for you but you keep on pushing—
Me back to the grave, untangle me like a rope
I cling into your lips like you're my only hope

-tick tack

We're a beautiful
catastrophe,
you and I

- ***catastrophe***

If your world becomes
a desert of snow,
I hope my love
is enough
to warm you

-desert of snow

In another universe, we held hands, walked the streets like nothing else mattered.

Calle Commercio was filled with pedestrians but your eyes lingered on me like I was the only one they see.

We explored the city of *Tuguegarao* as it offered us exhilarating adventures in the height of summer.

We stopped by *Huggamug Coffee Library,* traded tales of love and lost and thousand yearnings. I casted glimpses of you behind my thick lashes, blushed after I caught you casting glances too.

We filled the place with our laughter, played mind games while spilling coffee on the table. The fresh aroma of *Barako* filled the air but your scent occupied my mind, making me daze.

In another universe, we talked until 3 am about *everything*—Philosophy, History, Literature. We talked about school. I was glad we share the same views as regards policies. It was perfect, almost surreal.

You told me about where you came from—a passionate Northerner who settled here for adventure. You weathered storms, told me stories of how you endured unfavorable circumstances. They made you *dream*. Those hardships shaped your vision. You told me so much about yourself that I felt so close...so drawn to you. Every time you smile, I gravitated towards you like your twinkling eyes were magnets attracting me.

I relive these moments in my mind now as I lie here, on this cold ground, watching the constellations.

In another universe, we located *Cassiopeia*. Reminiscing the vain and boastful queen, we talked about the sacrificed maiden, *Andromeda* and how *Perseus* came to her rescue after she was chained to a rock—a pawn to monsters. You stared at me after that, fixed my stubborn strands with your hand and gazed deeper.

I didn't know what you saw, but you leaned to brush your lips against mine. It was a brief touch but almost felt infinite.

You told me in a hushed voice, *"If you will ever need me like Andromeda, I will always be here."* How secured that made me feel. How *blessed*. How *loved*. Until....

Our images disappeared like smoke, and I am back to our universe. I stare at the space you occupied in my reverie and could almost feel your warmth, the life inside of you rising up above, leaving me forever.

In another universe, we held hands. You were mine and I was yours.

In another universe, nothing else mattered.

In our universe, you won't even look at me.

In our universe, my existence doesn't even matter to you. I am insignificant.

In another universe...

-a reverie

Remember darling,
I am made of ice
So, if you are fire,
don't come near me

- ***ice and fire***

I want to be lost
in my ocean of thoughts,
linger in the depth
of my rambling chaos

Perhaps to be lost is better
than have me stand
in front of you
but never seen
For you seek
the comfort
of winding lies
not the beautiful fiasco
of black stormy hair,
freckled facial skin,
a pair of clear brown eyes
dancing about your face—
once in a while they stop
to stare
a little deeper
like they're trying to probe
into your soul
that is completely shrouded
in an exquisite smile:
a perfect masquerade

-*lost in the ocean of thoughts*

I try to know you
like a sacred creed
but you hide beneath
layers of cemented lies
You refuse to speak
to my exposed soul,
cast away the truth
back to the grave
where it spent
eons of incarceration
Why wouldn't you look at me
as I bare it all?
I stand in stark nudity
before you
but you turn away
Are you afraid
to discover what's engraved
in my bones
for so long?
Your name—
tattooed in me, in my soul
A beautiful calligraphy
of pain,
an anguished scream
swallowed by the wind,
a tale of love and lost
spilled carelessly
in ancient *Baybayin*

-*tattooed in me*

If you're not going to hold
me
like I'm going to fall,
we
will never collide
like soulmates ought to
baby!

-collide

First of all, I would like to say I'm sorry.

I'm sorry that I'm running away again. I'm running away after being slapped by the hand of rationality. Yes, you're sweet and romantic but I deserve so much more than the illusion you're trying to paint in my head with words I've grown accustomed to—such sweet words that do not possess a life of their own, bereft of the possibility of future realization. Somehow, they're just fragments of a promise, a hushed sound of uncertainty but were nevertheless uttered to feed the speaker's fancy. I'm yet to fall into such a romantic machination coming with the love bug crawling over my blanket. You have the audacity to say you love me but that's all. I've been waiting for the *things that you will do* to make me feel that that love is real and you're feeling it with every breath that you take.

Love—love isn't just a word you can say. It isn't something I can just believe in a dazed mind. *It's so much more*. It's a commitment that binds people for eternity, a sacred vow to hold two hearts together. It's not a game ought to be played or a fire that can easily be extinguished by tanks of water. It's not pupils dilating or tongues sprinkled with deathly dose of fructose, or a vision of the moon getting bigger in a glance.

It's a chance, *a one in a million chance,* a risk someone has to take willingly for no reason at all. Ours are just words you managed to weave to fill the vast spaces between us, words I can't simply take for they lack justification. Words without justification are merely claims, pieces of information that lack merit. You're sweet and gentle and kind *but deadly.*

Deadly because you make me want to fall without any assurance as to where I stand in your life. What am I to you to begin with? Just a girl you can show off to everyone like a trophy. Someone who walks and sits beside you so you won't be alone in a crowd.

You haven't defined the role I am playing but I am playing it anyhow, though I am always scared of breaking my heart yet again. So, before this gets deeper, I have to run away.

I'm sorry.

-undefined

People come,
people go
Some stay,
some fade away
But like the freckles
scattered on my face,
the emotions linger
They don't disappear
no matter how hard
I scrub
My skin becomes raw,
it bleeds
but my heart still drums
the way you made it
Oh, I hate
how you keep me enslaved
I wish the memories
that we shared
fade away
like scars lightening
with the touch
of lemon juice!

- *freckles scattered*

I don't know where to start
If I look into your eyes again,
I am afraid the spark
is gone
Just like the warmth
engulfing my skin
when we touch,
it has cooled
My love,
when we kiss,
I taste death on my lips
I wish to talk but I don't
know where to begin
so, I will just
drink silence in
like a morphine

-morphine

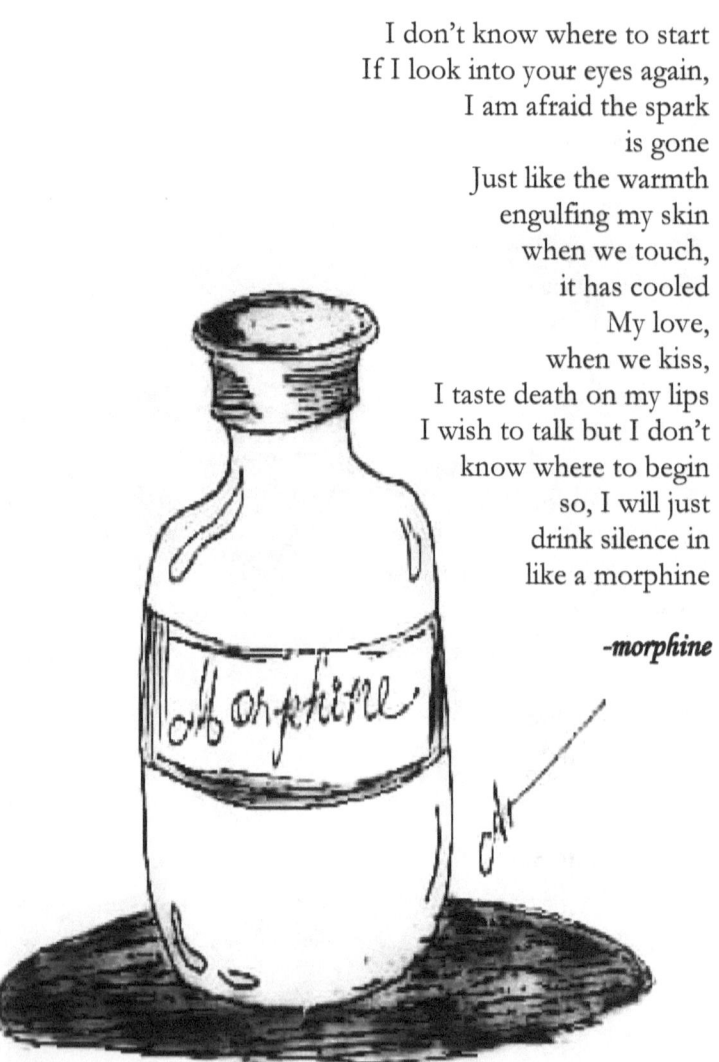

Now that you left
me heartbroken,
even silence
has a sound
Over my ears
it screams so loud
I can't bear
to hear
it reverberates
for the pain
drags me down
with the emptiness
gaining weight
with the liquid
rolling swiftly
on my face

- ***emptiness gaining weight***

In retrospect,
I'm beginning
to love
the bruises,
the cuts,
the knife stabs
on my back,
the pool
of blood
that drenched
your expensive
Persian rug,
the slashes
and the cracks
that you called
paper cuts

Oh, I'm beginning
to love
the wounds
you invalidated
with a shrug

-paper cuts

Is this really how healing
feels like?
For I—
I feel like losing
my humanity, I
am numb all over
The
pain
is
gone
along with
the passion,
the fresh blood dripping,
filling
the spaces inside my head
My heart is dead!
The words crawl back
to my pen, I
can no longer write
messy poems I
dare to call
art

-*how healing feels like*

I wear my heart on my sleeves as they taught me in my old town. Now I weep over torn letters, grieve over empty teacups, howl with the cold breeze. I fall with trembling knees; stretch myself across cold walls. I try to hold strangers, prevent them from falling apart like I am a thread that can sew broken fragments.

Sometimes I forget I am merely a woman who passed through a needle's eye. I kissed pretentious lips in an odd way, was in love but ran away. I swore not to be that naïve girl again. However, shadows chase me and I never really got the chance to change. Now I sit alone in this cafeteria, let my wandering mind slip through places I am no longer welcome so I can hear the words again—those magical words that used to warm my chest, *they are still there*. Sometimes they come back to haunt my mind.

I want to go back to that time when love was mine to command but I no longer belong there. I guess I am doomed to linger here, spend my whole life trying to hold the tears so the mascara I wear won't stain my ashen face.

-when love was mine to command

Our trains kept diverging as we go
Yet somehow, I always find
myself *returning home* to you

And you *shut the door* to my face
every time!

-*diverging fate*￼

You become the people that you meet. The words they speak will be your creed. The song they sing will be the lullaby that puts you to sleep. Where they touched you will bear a print, a tattoo to show how you've been held. How fingers clawed your skin until you're etched from within—you will crave it every time you feel empty. Your body will remember and you will never be the same again. You will feel a void in places where warmth used to be.

You become the people that you follow. When confused, your eyes will scan footsteps before you. These footsteps may lead you to rivers, some to unknown meadows. Others pave way to deserts, some will take you to the woods where many have wandered and got lost. There are also those that will lead you to the dreams you sketched in your mind, prints that will show you the right direction like a compass. Be careful as you choose. The risk is too great to just leap. Before you take that first step, consider what I've said: *You become the people that you meet; you become the people that you choose to follow.*

-become the people that you meet

Darling, how
can you *sleep*
so soundly
knowing I
am *bleeding,*
screaming,
shattering?

-soundly

You built a roof
over my head,
built a fence
so high
that I can't glimpse
beyond
You fed
me fables
with a silver spoon
My hunger
was quenched,
strength
returning
I was ready to
believe in love *again*

But the roof
that you built
started crumbling
with the high fence
as you spit
venom into my lips
and everything
became vivid!

-roof over my head

"You're *beautiful when you smile*", he murmured, his eyes focused on hers as though trying to capture all of her in his mind. Dark strands fell into a storm of waves framing her face in a picturesque of total mess and beauty. She shook her head gently and met his gaze. "No. I am beautiful when I break.", she replied. "When trapped in a desert with my demons, and my pieces try to turn the place over for an oasis, I feel beautiful. People miss that all the time. How well my suppressed cries rhyme with the sound of my brittle bones breaking—an eggshell rapidly cracking under the weight of a rock. How I cast my fury with the sand storm, burn the arid ground with my heated glances also add up to things that make me beautiful.

"It's a sight to behold but people don't look at those things. No one wants to look at cracks and creases and wounds and bruises, *and I am unapologetically made of these*. People want perfection and a single flaw is enough to distort an image; dismiss it as hideous and unworthy. Much more a woman of shattered pieces bleeding ceaselessly.

"No, I don't think I am beautiful when I smile so mystically like my lips has been bestowed an honor to be touched by the tip of Da Vinci's brush. I am not beautiful when my eyes glisten with the galaxies as a ray of sunshine passes through them in a microsecond, too fast that it seems surreal, like the glow never reached the soul hidden behind the twinkling retinas. I am not beautiful when I walk so gently, my movements jive perfectly with my chiffon dress in a dance that makes a poet wants to immortalize me with the daffodils. Even as a puff of zephyr brushes my hair, and my cheeks flush color that matches the splendid sunset, I am far from beautiful. Never in that faint shimmer of *perfection*.

"I am not beautiful with those moments heightened with incredible mirth. For when toned down, I can't even hear an echo or see a print. Moments like those are evanescent, and what I have will never commensurate with them in any way. I prefer to linger and agonize with infinite time.

"No. I am not beautiful when I smile. I am not beautiful when you look at all the angles that frame my face. Perfection evades me like chances fleeting with the hand of the clock. I am beautiful in my chaos, in my cracks, in my private grief. I am beautiful in places no one dares to look. And that, my friend is the reason why even if you are beholding me right now, everything else is vague and *you're not really seeing me*.

'Not at all. "

-beautiful in places no one dares to look

Are

    grown ups

        supposed

            to feel

              this

      m   e   s   s   e   d

              up?

            -grown ups

Sometimes, I feel like my mind is divided into compartments, each containing my shattered parts captured in a memory, a dream, or a lost intensified by a yearning I managed to lock in a jar, along with wishes I whispered to the stars. Some of these compartments contain a shimmer of remorse, some highlighted by a brief encounter with love which I used to regard as lasting but turned out to be ephemeral. There are also those scattered with scoops of faith—that one word that has kept me unbending. Then, there's that compartment filled with my darkness. I tossed it in the labyrinth for fear that it will rise up like a Minotaur.

These compartments are strictly separated from each other by a carbon steel to ensure they won't meet or engulf one another in their own private mess, no matter how intense the pressure. For in between them, I keep *you*, the most valued proof of my existence. I'll make sure you won't come across with any of my unsightly parts. My greatest fear is for you to stumble along my unpolished sides, got pricked and run scared. Though part of me longs for you to unwrap me terrified yet humbled by my own imperfections, I dread the moment when you'd get swallowed by my angry storm.

So, I promise to hold you in a safe compartment so you will be protected from the ***sharp edges of my broken soul.***

How is it possible

for someone to feel

intact while breaking;
healed while bleeding;
dauntless while scared;
composed while freaking out?

-*someone to feel*

Some people stay
not because they still care
but because,
>	*THEY PROMISED.*

"Show me your darkness!" he said. "All of it. I want to see how deep it goes. Roar your thunder, fuse with evil. Make me feel how cruel your heart can become when pierced in tatters. Kiss me when you're cold, envelope me in your wrath. I dare you to remove the mask you're wearing; expose me to your naked soul. Allow me to discover everything that has hurt, maimed and made you, *you*.

I did not come here to simply feast on the beauty designed to lure me. Don't take it the wrong way. I confess, your smile captivates me every time—a temptation I can't resist. Your lingering glances give me premature ventricular contractions. You are the most sinfully attractive person my eyes have ever seen but I want to look beyond what physicality can offer. I want to see you bereft of all that flashes of beauty. I want to hear how fierce you can swear; taste how bitter you can lie. Show me how vulnerable you can be when faced with the things that scare you. Meet me in your rawness. If it's not asking too much."

So, I looked him in the eyes, slowly unleashed my demons and let them dance with him.

-*in your rawness*

One of the shittiest things that can happen
in life is watch someone you loved fulfill
all the dreams you talked about

      WITH *SOMEONE ELSE.*

I want to talk about the roses you never learned to like. Those roses so red, they looked like dripping blood. Yes, I sent them—a bouquet that won't paint a smile on your lips or cause a shimmer of mirth in your eyes. I know you won't even smell them. *It's okay.* I want you to know I understand. *And I am sorry.*

I am sorry I was *too late*. I am sorry I was able to look into your eyes without seeing your pieces breaking. I am sorry I endured listening to the odes you recited without caring to drink in the meaning behind the rhymes. I am sorry I thought I loved you so much, *I did not believe you can still feel empty inside.* I am sorry I laughed when you told me you will cut yourself that night. I was so insensitive. I am sorry I ignored the message you sent to my cellphone because,

> *I was so busy picking*
> *red roses*
> *you NEVER LEARNED to like!*

Now you're gone and I never really thought you will haunt me even in dreams.

I am sorry…

-roses you never learned to like

I met myself in a dream,
she was panting in exhaustion
Her eyes that were usually bright
were dull from the tears blinding them
I took her in my arms,
tried to comfort her with words
She sobbed like a child,
warned me of the future
She said, *"Take care of your heart.*
Train it to withstand
the strongest storm.
For I tried so hard
but failed,
thought razor blades
were the answer."

I looked into her
bloodshot eyes,
felt death crawled
against my skin

It was then that I realized
I wasn't in a dream
but in my funeral!

-met myself in a dream

There are days when I can't answer the phone. *Forgive me* for my days aren't always filled with rays of sunshine. It's raining too hard, most of the time. Other times, it's snowing that I stay with the crowd to keep warm.

I would leave the heater on at home so when I arrive during evenings, I won't be engulfed in the cold. I would open the door slowly so the slight creak won't wake the household I don't have. I would curve my lips into a smile, make a cup of coffee, watch the news of the day and *think*.

I would think of happier moments, of happier places and thousands of reasons why they sped away like bullet trains bounded somewhere I cannot be. When it's time for bed, I would take my favorite book with me, gather all the pillows around and try to lose my mind in different dimensions—somewhere I think I might belong, a quiet place everyone has abandoned. A memory would up; something I have been keeping for years. I would freeze it for a couple of minutes, savor the waves of nostalgia, and try to fall asleep.

I would wrap myself in a blanket as tears begin to rock my exhausted body. When the pain intensifies, I would curse the gods so loudly. The phone would ring from across the room. Lethargic, I won't pick it up. So it would fill the whole house with its hollow screams that send me to the zenith of my depression.

Forgive me. It's a struggle every day. It's not anyone else's fault that I roll myself in the grave, point a finger in the air, blame someone imaginary. When sleep finally takes me into its arms, I would cling to it like a lover I never want to lose. I would beseech the gods to show mercy and kill me in my sleep. *They won't.*

Tomorrow, I would wake to a harrowing silence broken by the eerie sound of the telephone. It would ring insistently for hours, tempting me to pick up. *Forgive me.* I don't think I would answer even then.

-answer the phone

When she's bleeding hard,
don't run away
The night may be too cold
but it won't last long!

-last long

What makes you think
to be lost is a misery?

Don't you know
it's a journey?

A journey where
a faint possibility
is paved

A possibility
that somewhere
along the endless passage
of time,
you could be found

If you could not be,
then maybe
you're meant
to make it home
ALONE

-to be lost

You claw burrows on earth looking for planted clues that may lead you to the next me. You miss the little storm of thoughts I brought that lazy afternoon when we played logic over coffee. You dig my eloquence from every stranger you collide, none of which resembles the soul I now hide.

Haven't I told you I am a package deal? That I've got heaven and hell swirling above me while I sit on purgatory with a cup of freshly brewed coffee? I guess you missed all of that for you busied yourself with your fantasies while I was there with you. Now you look for me everywhere, *the one who got away*. Baby, it saddens me to say, you can spend eternity looking but I'm the last of my kind.

-last of my kind

People take their lovers
to the movie theaters
so, they can watch
them gush over
their favorite film

-movie theaters

This may sound a little heart wrenching but breaking down at 2 AM changes you. You become distant. You become doubtful. It creates an emotional divide between you and people. When you're slumped on the floor, paralyzed with grief, you begin to see through things. The Niagara of tears falling from your eyes, the lump in your throat, the pain pounding in your chest remind you of the faces you want to see, the voices you want to hear, the caresses you want to feel. You become isolated.

It's 2 AM, the world turns against you, the clock ticks louder than it used to as though to match the shrieking voices in your head. Those voices you wish would fall into silence for they drive you mad. You reach for your phone, type a text, try to dial a number, then change your mind. You begin to think of coping mechanisms. How do you get through this? Swallow a sleeping pill that doesn't work anymore? Seek the comfort of alcohol? Dance with your demons, let them torment you until you become numb? You become lost. You don't know what to do. You pinch your skin to drive away the numbness. Everything becomes blurry. In a brief moment of clarity, he crosses your mind; you're tempted to phone him. *You need him.* You've told him about this before. He said he loves you but never called. He slept while you're breaking so why bother at all? *Why bother?*

This may sound a little heart wrenching but breaking down at 2 AM changes you. It makes you question the people in your life. Don't they care enough to check on you? You've always been there for people but when you need them, they're not available. And that special someone who told you he'll stick around, why can't you tell him you're depressed? Why can't you tell him you're breaking down again? Because he didn't seem to care the last time you opened up. So, you swore not to bother him from then on. Then you begin to distrust his intentions. You begin to see flaws in his personality. You begin to bring up issues that drive him to the wall. You become the toxic person you always hated. You long to be understood but you can't even understand yourself anymore. You become the riddle. You become the freak.

-breaking at 2am

I wish I could just fall
and ***cry me a river.***

But I won't.

For if I do,
there's no one I could call

NO ONE AT ALL!

To have a heart,
is both a blessing
and a curse
For this organ
that pumps blood,
just keeps wanting
someone it should not
When I told
it to stop,
I got a punch in the gut—
so hard that it took
me 461 sols
to recover

-sols to recover

I smoked all the weeds,
swallowed all the booze
Yet my senses still throb
in cadence with the tone
of my terrifying storm,
swirling emotions
that remind me of summer—
of you
and all of the painful reasons
I have to let you go
I watched you walked
out of that door
while I talked
about sunsets and all
of our broken hopes
scattered in wild extremes
You didn't turn when I broke,
shattered like a figurine,
melted on the floor
Your face danced on the ceiling,
I can't even cry enough
I still hold tears within,
prevent them to flow,
and drown me while I scream

-all the painful reasons

The truth
is that we're all scarred
So, we crawl under
a blanket of lies
to conceal ***who we are***

What if one day, we wake up and find out that everything we ever had—the laughter shared, the late-night talks, even the times when we were too dazed to realize we're falling in love weren't real? That the hand I held in mine, the face that looked divine, the kiss that was more intoxicating than wine were just products of an illusion staged to make us *believe there is love?*

What if there is no love in reality? That the web of magical emotions we think we feel is actually a concept put forth in another universe; a concept too complex to be derived in ours. Would you still be brave to look me in the eyes? If I won't be able to utter a word, would you still trust in promises? Or you would just fall asleep and dream with me. Because in dreams, it is easier to believe in anything. There's no need of a hologram projector to show an illusion of love.

I need to know, baby. Love for me is just another theory like Singularity, White Holes and Black Holes. I would like to know if it's something you would give your time to prove so we can decide right now whether or not our hearts have a place to call home.

-*a theory to prove*

Your lips move
in a gentle cadence,
urging mine
to join the dance
There is no music
just our hearts
echoing to the beat
of the universe
as it vibrates
in an endless cacophony,
reminding how our souls
are connected
since the beginning of time
You trace the shadows
cast in my face
like you're trying to rearrange
my chaos with your gaze
I am lost at the moment
as you love me beneath
my flesh and bones
Your kisses fill me
with ethereal songs
I move with you in frenzy,
still too dazed to speak
then suddenly you wake me
from my dreamless sleep

-ethereal song

My young heart bleeds words it cannot speak. *What is the reward for loyalty?*

Deceit? All the pains I have to endure? Oh, I weep for another shattered dream as I sit watching all the castles you built in the air.

I admit, I have my own shortcomings. There are days, when I preferred running, frightened of your warmth, overwhelmed by your tenderness. But those days when I ran, I've always sought you like a plant needing the light of the sun. I always found myself retracing the steps back to you. *Always back to you.*

Yes, I have my shortcomings. There are moments when I questioned the depth of your love, like a convict questioning the wisdom behind the law that indicted him. I let silence wrap me, comforted by its deafening scream. I loved you—even the moon blushed when I tried to get this truth out of my chest. Oh, it melted me, as my heart became colder than liquid hydrogen. Seven hells— I was trapped in one of these for the longest time. I gave up the will to live; befriended death in my solitude. I let darkness swallow me, fill me with its wrath. In the pangs, you found me. Like a Seraphim's sigh, your voice woke me up and I was reborn.

I offered you my all, gave you all the love in the world. I fell deeper for you even when everyone advised me against it. I followed my heart as it led me to a battle I did not prepare myself for—an open combat where I lost every time. I did not care. *For I loved you so much.*

You took advantage of that. My love, you cut me so deep, maimed me ruthlessly. You severed every artery, watched me bleed to death. In the verge of it all, loyal I remained.

But what is the reward for loyalty?

Your cold kiss? Hands of deceit holding me closer than phantoms ever did? Tears luring me back to sleep? Pains sending me back to the cave of broken promises?

I remained true even when I wasn't sure of how you felt. I gambled.

What is the reward for loyalty?

Her arms closely wrapped in your arms last September first?!

-*september first*

How can you
say, *"I love you!"*
then watch my wrath
incinerate me into
insignificant ash?
Baby, I am corroding
before your eyes!
How can you bear
the smell of rotting
flesh mixing
with tears and kerosene?

-corroding before your eyes

The day it started raining, she tried to roast her coffee.

(Someone told her it would taste better.)

While it really did, the bile rising from her throat prevented her from swallowing.

So, she spit it out,
        watched the aromatic liquid hit
the white wall standing between
              her and the rain,

and thought of him.

-between her and the rain

Time does not soothe
burns, it does not work
to make pains
disappear
It passes by,
we had it all wrong
The ancient wisdom
lied to us all
Time—
can never be tamed
so, the parts of me
that cried
after you put out
the fire
will be screaming
for eternity
For time
does not heal
our broken hearts
like we have been told

-*about time*

There's an irony
that makes the laughter
cringe with the sea breeze
reaching
my nostrils
as I yield
to the tantalizing
view,
eyes searching
for a faint sign
of you
You're not there
The bitterness resounding
from the piano
says it all
I had my shot,
tried to hold you
as you sat
beside me
while I played
a sad song
for your wedding day

-a sad song

Sadness dripping
in my blood kills
all of my dreams
I sing
with the daffodils
Oh, you wrap yourself
in a blanket
as I scream
Remember the time
when I asked
you to love me deeper
when I'm sad?

Why did you sleep
soundly while I bleed?
Do lies taste better
darling,
when the love is dead?

-lies taste better in death

Words escaping
your lips,
they wound
my skin
Now I am
scarred all over
I don't mind
though I still
wish Cupid
has a conscience
and that
we *didn't happen*
It's too late
for regrets
Too late to contest
all the arguments escaping
from your tongue
So, allow me to
thank you
for the tragedy!

Let's write something
that doesn't involve guns
and blood,
too much yelling I
cover my ears with lies
The world is a *better place*—
always a better place to die in!
All I see are graveyards
stretching far and wide
like stars plotted in a chaotic sky
Oh, I sigh,
believing all the lies
uttered so we can survive
the night
while thunderous bombs
resound here and there,
fallen bodies scattered
everywhere
Maybe I—
I will let you speak
about love to me tonight
It doesn't matter now if you'll lie
we will die sooner or later
you and I
So, let's drink to all the fallen souls,
wrap our hearts with steel
while we profess love,
such a foreign emotion
we can't even fathom
We say it anyhow like it's as nonsense
as the war going on

I will let you sprinkle each word
with sugar so, they'll taste sweet
if I roll them on my tongue
and say them back to you—
a response
that could melt glaciers
perhaps in a different time
Tonight may only be
the chance left for us
So, what are you waiting for,
lie to me
Let's stage the greatest farce
in this time of war

We'll be the great pretenders,
you and I

-chaotic sky

How could the eyes that graced
my naked body got scared
of the soul I bared
in my last attempt
to be understood?

-naked soul

Perhaps I am cursed
to fall in love
with the moon,
admire its phases: *crescent*
or whole
as I scribble
letters
I will never send

Maybe I'm destined
to write poetry for free
and the feelings that linger
after I finish a piece
will only collide with
the silent sobs
I've yet to release
trapped in the ruins
of *you and me*

-poetry for free

Don't ask the moon
what phase she's in
You promised a love
that will hold her
when she falters,
a love that won't shatter bones
pierce flesh,
or watch blood gushes—
a stream of life escaping
vows turning into regrets
collapsing with the shadows
and tears shrouding her
Don't ask her to come out
when she hides behind the clouds
You promised a love
that will see her
through the darkness,
eyes beholding her weakness
like an art
clinging to the branches
swinging,
dancing
as the wind howls
She struggles to shine
Don't forget her
when your eyes
burn from lights way brighter
than she is when she's full
Don't forsake her
when she's eclipsed
You promised a love

that isn't ephemeral,
a love that transcends

           her simmering rage—
          rage that intensifies
         while she's caged
      in her betraying nature
      She wants to be full—
        full of light for you
          but she's meant
        to undergo phases
      You promised to love
        all of these phases
      that constantly shape
       her into crescents,
        always changing
     that you're squeezed,
trapped between the urge
     to flee or to linger
          It's difficult
          for the moon
       is not as constant
    as the air you breathe
    Sometimes she's whole,
     sometimes she breaks
         Yet no matter
     what phase she's in
she always tries to illuminate
       the way for you
     so, you won't stumble
           as you go
         Don't ask her

what phase she's in
tonight
Just love the moon
as fiercely as you would
a priceless art

-don't ask the moon what phase she's in

The rooftop where we fell in love that starry night of June 16, it awaits our return like flowers do for spring.

My feet, as though they have a mind of their own, led me there this afternoon. As I mounted the rusty iron stairway, your face kept floating before me like you're there, *waiting for me*. A distant memory occupied my mind and I couldn't help but smile at the vision of a *sweet, agonizing* **past I** would give my life to live again.

The first thing I noticed were the prints we made. They were still there, scattered at every corner like ghosts that refuse to abandon the place filled with *us*. They remind me that some things never change. I let out a short chuckle for the truth that I miss you so much dawned on me while I stood at the very space we occupied that night. Flashes of images came rushing back, making me nostalgic of a night I buried a long time ago. We were young—way too young to understand what *love is*. But we took the risk, didn't we? We braved the uncertainties. We were happy. *Do you remember?*

Oh, how *I remember everything:* the details of your face, the creases on your forehead as you fathomed the wisdom behind Quantum Mechanics. I was seated in front of you, absorbing your enigmatic soul. I *was seventeen* but my heart, though young and naive and free, *was sure of you.*

And as I watched you frown over your notes, trying to make sense of those mathematical formulas spilled carelessly on the pages, my heart swelled in my chest, every frenzied beat spoke your name.

Baby, I remember how we gambled over shooting stars which, at that moment, were miraculously raining from the night sky. You told me in between our animated talks, "If I see five shooting stars tonight, you're mine."

I smiled at you. We just witnessed the first one fall. Honestly, I never believed in signs or destiny. Much more in a wish granted by a shooting star. You were too confident in your words while I muttered silly under my breath. For hours, we talked about Galileo, the epic of Sundiata, Newton and Gravity. *No shooting stars. No sign. Nothing.* So, we went on talking about ancient Sumer. I talked about Sundial and how it was used to tell time. I glanced at my watch that read 11:30. *Still, no shooting star.* We talked about our dreams. You told me about your childhood. I was fascinated by the vastness of your memory. And just before you started talking about the beauty that was the night, *shooting stars started falling.*

We counted six. Sealed it with a kiss.

Do you remember? From that night, we kept returning to that rooftop. We filled every corner of it with memories; both *blissful and painful memories*. And this afternoon, as I stood alone at the center, I could almost hear our voices. Those young lovers' whispers that has haunted me in years. The way you said *"I love you"* as you traced the angles of my face resounds in my head like a spell meant to strike me down. I know it's silly to still taste the bitterness of the dead promises. Time heals everything, they said. Well, how long has it been?

Nine?

Ten?

Eleven?

Twelve years! It has been twelve years but I still remember everything like it was only yesterday when I last held your hands. Unfortunately, the years have not been able to erase what we had, *who you were* to me. Time rolled by, changing us, but a part of you remained. In all those years of being apart, I carried you in my heart.

I remember. Everything. I know you are happy now. You are with someone who truly deserves you. *It could have been me. It was one decision away from being me.* There were times when I regretted not choosing to stay. Until now, it still pierces my heart. But you know, at that moment, I was free to make a choice, free to make a reality for both of us. Yes, I was blinded by love, driven by fear of losing you. Yet even in the verge of my madness, the gods bestowed me a brief moment of lucidity. I saw how miserable you were with me. That fact has killed me a thousand times more than our parting.

You are the most precious person I've ever met. It pained me to be the one wrecking you. So, I chose to set you free.

I hope you realize I did it because I loved you so much. I went back to that rooftop to spill the truth.

I deemed it proper to finally have a closure in the place where we fell in love to free it from our memories, to free myself from guilt.

I hope, you have forgiven me.

-*rooftop*

Words crowding my mind,
screaming out rage confined
beneath stone cold flesh—
a chaotic sky
rolling clouds of memories
into oblivion

-memories rolling into oblivion

I run away
escaping
dark shadows
rising
chasing
me everywhere—
unforgiving
storms
determined
to squeeze
the remaining
ounces of
strength
in my veins
I flee as fast as I can
from the scattered
remnants
of my shattered soul
But how can I
escape
from all of these
shadows
when the truth
is they're here
residing
inside my head?

-escape the chaos

But I loved you,
my darling
When I tied
your shoelaces
in an effort
to hold
your pieces intact
in my hands
while the world around you
didn't seem to care
if you break
or lose yourself
to the night,
I was there
I wish
your heart
can remember
me and that moment
before February ends...

-that moment before february

Thank you for setting me free, for choosing to let go, for giving up on me. You know how I broke the moment your footsteps died in the hall. Tore my heart out when the truth that we're finally over dawned. I was desperate, crying for hours over a love I thought would last. For weeks I kept imploring the gods. In grief, I was begging you to come back.

Then suddenly, I was no longer grieving. Suddenly, I was no longer pained. Suddenly, I was no longer mumbling your name.

For in the darkness, he found me. Brave as Lochinvar, he took my hand. Suddenly, I am looking at the sunset. Suddenly, I notice his eyes are golden. Suddenly he becomes my one and only. Suddenly, he means the world to me.

-he means the world to me

It's time to go.

How I hate the sound of my footsteps against the tiled floor, the fading hues, the melancholic blast of wind, all of which are as cold and as dead as my heart. I really tried to warm it when you're near but to no avail.

It's not the same, baby. *Nothing's the same.* I cling to the promises we made, yes—all dead words that escaped deaf walls and ceilings, and crept somewhere beneath my skeleton dreams.

I try to swim to the surface, though the weight of the words remain unspoken between us drags me to the bottom of this unknowable lake where I am trapped with you.

I hate to break free from your arms but how could I stay when they already turned into ropes binding me into a pillar of futile wishes? Whatever happened to the home I used to love with all my heart? Everything just turned into dust I can't even bury myself with.

So, it's time to go.

-*dead words*

Now that I've told you,
what you mean to me
I can go...
go where my pains walk,
a one-way street
disappearing into
the dark undertow
of swirling emotions
that drag me below
I can't swim to the surface
for the weight
tied around my feet
is too heavy
I can't speak
for the lump
in my throat is bigger
than my fear of being lost
with the miasma
surrounding me
I am glad
I was bestowed
with a chance
to tell you something
I felt a long time ago
I love you
Now that you know,
heard from my lips
that you mean
the universe to me,
I can go,
flee with the night

to somewhere
your heart cannot follow
for it's cold and my heart
freezes December over
as it dies with the sun
I can't warm you there
so, stay,
stay right here
where the stars shine down
on your face and wrap you
with the sweet
confessions of love
I bravely spilled
Oh, I hope
what we had is enough
to sustain you
until fate decides
to send me home again
to you…

-where the stars shine down

"If I fall, tell Helen... tell her...."

If I fall, tell him...
well, how does
death romanticize love?
How does love
incorporate itself
into someone's last breath?
Through an anguished sigh?
A faint glimmer in the eye?
A whispered goodbye?
I don't know how
Maybe a futile wish?
A quick last kiss?
Or a word that will appease
the grieving soul before it falls
to its knees
That must be it!
I can't clearly fathom though
what you shall tell him
I'll leave it to you
Just make sure
that as you breathe
words you choose to speak,
he will feel me between the syllables
like I'm there, **cradling him close**
in my dying heartbeat

In all those times that I lived, all I've ever written were elegies for the love I used to feel for you but died tragically. It died tragically after you left me with open wounds that won't mend; bruised me with words way too abusive, they make me shake uncontrollably even now. And your memory, the face that resembles the moon, it haunts me. It haunts me that I run away from the crowd as if I'm losing my mind. The cacophony gets louder and your voice, I hear it over the hubbub swallowing me. You call me like you still own all of me. *Oh, I confess, you still do my darling, you still do.* Though I claim that my love has died a long time ago, it throbs with the heart you occupied. You scarred my skin with your name so I will remember you for eternity. I will surely remember you for you gave me so much to remember.

I know you're gone but my pen just can't stop writing about you. So, I write another piece...another cold work of art. For the twenty-seventh time, here's to the love I want to shower you with but has to die because you left before I can even offer my heart to you. Now I am here, staring at a blank space that used to be our home.

Oh darling, why does love have to be so cold?

-*for all the things that refuse to die*

Though my mind is fragmented,
I don't consider it a curse
because through its brokenness,
light passes through
In between fragments,
my art exists,
a faint shimmer
fighting its way
towards recognition

Someday, the world will
know of its greatness

-fragmented

I tried to vomit you
but my mouth held you back,
swallowed you—
a mixture of bitterness
and love
A qualm swirling me about,
you're within me, a part of me
Even when I close my eyes
I see you,
a pair of expressive brown eyes
smiling at me as I curse
the heavens
I want to untangle you
from my soul
Why can't I baby?
Why can't you
just leave
and consider this
our last kiss?

What if everything
we ever put forth:
laws, numbers,
all theories and letters
are just faint sketches
of something which
existence is rather unfathomable
even to the brightest of all minds
We—you and me,
of all entities
floating like a gigantic disc
across the realm
of time and space
are the greatest farce
ever staged
in the history creation

-faint sketches

I rewrote the stars
in my last attempt
to make you fall
Well, you did fall
irrevocably
in her arms
Seems like fate
is really against me
after all!

-last attempt

Love me on ordinary days: when the sky is grey and I am silent in a corner, trying hard not to cry. It may not be the best sight to behold in a day, but it is when I need your arms the most. So, pull me closer, lock me into that warm embrace not because it's my birthday or the wind feels insanely cold like December, but because I am breaking in a rapid avalanche, all the emotions bottled are finding their way out. My heart, though it beats weakly, it is full of hope that the grey sky will turn bright again, and we can lie on our backs to watch the stars again. Love me when I can't even have faith with the fading hues. Be here with me, hold me as I weep because your touch makes everything feels easier. Your hands can lift my burden like a feather. I don't know how you do that. It enthralls me that you feel like my silver lining.

My blue sky.
My home.

Love me on ordinary days: when bouquet of Roses becomes cliché and the world only showers affection on Valentine's Day. For even sweet nothings are slowly fading as people have grown weary of love songs. It's getting cold, hearts are slowly turning into steel, and I am painfully dying inside. Look me in the eye for your gaze melts the ice engulfing my soul, making me bereft of feelings, making me neglect the essence of standing here with you, watching the bustling metropolis throbs with life and dreams and thousand promises.

Love me on ordinary days: when my hideous smile tries to hide the lies and the grief that comes after an awkward goodbye, and all my fragile sighs, those sounds I make in the dark, they give away my inhibitions, crack my protective shell so that I am exposed with my stark nudity. In those moments I try to elope with negativity, catch me. Don't hesitate to hold me. I may be as stubborn as hell but I will listen to your voice for you always silence me like no one could. You always stop me from running scared. *You. My safe haven.* So, call my name and I will hear you over the cacophony.

Love me on ordinary days. Listen to the fragile sounds of my heart shattering and *know that as it breaks into pieces, into thousand shrieking wishes, it bears your name.* Pick me up piece after piece. Scope me in your arms and make me whole again. Expunge those howling sounds that make me fragile as a glass, and make me believe in happy endings. Restore my faith again. Make me the child who believes in promises again.

Love me on ordinary days. Under the grey sky, against the storm and the pouring rain, *love me*. I could not ask for anything more appropriate.

Just love me.

-*fragile sounds*

How can someone
who never stayed
feel so homesick
of his temporary home?
The flowing language,
all the songs
come back in ripples
filling the void
with flashes of colors,
a scent that reminds him
he belongs
But he never stayed
so how could
a part of him
linger there
like all this time
he never really left?

-homesick

Surprisingly, we were able to bond as though we are not ice and fire to begin with. I hope when the time comes and one of us is destroyed by the other, we won't be quick to judge, we won't be too hasty to generalize. Nature made us who we are and to be condemned because of it is like being questioned as to why we existed in the first place. When someone asks why you're here, it's okay to provide an answer. But when the world throws dagger at you for merely being here, that freaking hurts. Especially when the heart of such atrocity can be traced back to living your true nature.

No one should be condemned because of his nature. *If you're an ice, stay cold. If you're fire, burn.* If you choose to come together despite of differences, accept the consequences. It's that simple.

**-*nature*ID*

She can't even cry
over the words spilling
rain of daggers
against her skin,
wounding
the soul she's trying
to revive from slumber

-cry over words

When you smoked
the last stick of cigarette
and I still did not walk
into the room,
would you start dialing
my number?
Would you try
to call me,
am I home,
or anywhere near?
You need me there
You need my arms
around your neck
while you bet against death
Would you send a text?
Or you will just consume
the last stick
and forget
that I even exist

-*last stick*

But where can I hide
when my tormentor *resides
inside my mind*?

Did the words you spit on my tongue have thorns?
For they got stuck in my throat,
now I'm gagging from my own
lies spilling all over the carpeted floor!

-words stuck

I shall not speak of love again. Such burning flame I held so dear and believed in. In the end though, it just turned to be the thing that consumed me, diminished me into a hopeless romantic who persistently wishes she has never known love but bleeds hundred million stories about it.

-hundred million stories

Someday, you will fall in love and it's not going to be the feeling you've grown accustomed to. Those years filled with wild butterflies? Bouquet of roses? Spark in the eyes? All sweet nothings that send you to cloud nine? No, it's not going to be that. Your next love story will be a *mess*. A total mess. It will look like a tornado has passed and disarranged everything in your life. You will begin to question all that you ever believed in. You will begin to weigh what's worth your time and what's not.

But you will be strong.

This kind of love will make you strong. It will cause you to scream at the top of your lungs in the middle of the night when you have nothing left to give. It will make you doubt every promise that has ever said in the name of passion or commitment. You will uncover lies under beautiful flashes of skin and smiling faces that look like a dream. It will make you cringe against a gust of wind coming from an open window. It will make you bleed but it won't leave you weak. It will make you strong and you will appreciate it more than anything in this world. The moment this kind of love finds its way to your heart, you will be the bravest person ever lived. All because you will be able to handle it.

-not your usual love

How do we grieve
a loss so the pain
can flow
with the tears
to our pillow
and linger there
for a while
until the anguish
subsides?
How do we grieve
emptiness
so, it won't
weigh us down
to the burrow?
How do we grieve?
How do we move on
when loving what
was lost
is the only thing
we know?

-how do we grieve

But forgetting
is not my thing
I erase everything—
the songs we used
to sing,
the dreams
Oh, I try
to run away
from the shadows
that bear semblance
to the eyes that are
as warm as the summer sun,
floating carelessly
in my mind,
taking me back
to the moment when love
was ours to command
But darling, you are
scarred in my soul, I can't
make you fade
no matter how hard I scrub
My skin becomes red and raw
I try
but forgetting, it eludes me
Now I'm crying
over the spoil
of what could have been
a story
worth *remembering*

-forgetting

Sometimes I have to bleed silently for even when your hands catch droplets of my blood, you just shrug your shoulder and walk away.

Sometimes I want to ask you why you ignore me when I'm hurting. But most often than not, I find it more convenient to just break at the corner. *Silently.*

Maybe I am made to endure the pain alone. Maybe my heart and bones are stronger than anyone else's.

Maybe…

-*stronger heart*

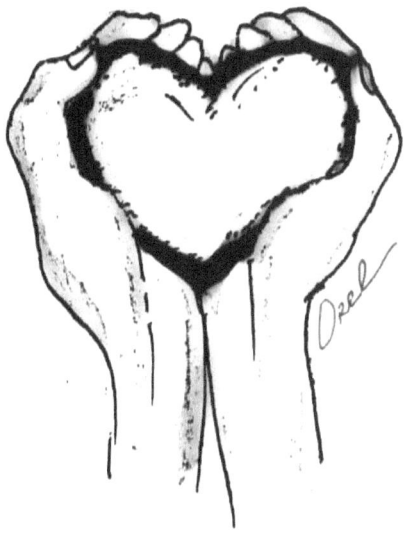

Even the summer heat
could not melt
the ice hugging
my heart
I'm too cold,
too numb
to be alive
Free me with a kiss
Maybe your lips
could light up the fire
that was once alive
in my veins
but has turned
into a smoke
suffocating me

-turned into smoke

In previous lifetime,
I fell in love with a song—
a melody filling my head,
a fresh wind gusting
making my hammock swing
in perfect rhythm with the leaf
sprouting to welcome spring

As the lyrics harmonized
with the butterflies in my chest,
I saw him standing there,
a misty apparition
eclipsing the sun in the horizon
My heart throbbed erratically
as the wind blew his scent—
a musky, masculine scent
filling my head like a drug

I inhaled all of him
until I am intoxicated
and when I was completely wasted
he disappeared to the forest

-completely wasted

What if?
What if the devil only sinned
because he's trapped from within
All the echoes of his screams
are swallowed by the wind
And then he fell
into her arms
Well, who could tell?
He felt something stir
from the heart
he thought was dead

What if?
What if the devil only sinned
because he was destined
to commit such a grave wrong
so, he can craft his song,
offer it to her
in exchange of her
captivating glances
smile that burns distances,
arms that extend bridges
from heaven to hell
Well, who could tell?
In love, he fell

What if?
What if the devil only sinned
just so he could win
over what his heart
screams from the start

and he can't listen now
to all the demeaning howls,
curses from his brothers
branding him an outcast
Driven away from hell,
made to endure time on earth
with the human he fell in love with
oh, how he misses home
but he can't go back
Now he's stuck
with humanity
All he knows is enmity
He needs to survive

Now, what if
What if the devil only sinned
to survive
in a world
in a heart
in a destiny
he can't even
claim his

-the devil only sinned

The world is my nemesis. It rips me apart. So, I will tell you today. *I will tell you today.* Tomorrow's a blur— a vague possibility. By then, who knows, I might disappear with the shadows.

It has to be today. Words, I will roll them on the tip of my tongue. Rehearsing in front of my mirror, I watch how my cheeks flash colors for the first time.

Today. It has to be today. I will tell you today. So, I open my mouth, force myself to speak. *You're not here.* You disappeared. So, the words, I swallow them back.

I hope that I'll die with them as I curse the clock.

-nemesis

My mind is a messy place,
a dangerous place
and I am trapped inside it everyday
I watch the hand of the clock
moves with the clouds,
feel moments fleeting
while I grab a pen
to scribble the chaos
turning my head
into a hose spilling rambles
on the wall,
on the ceiling,
all over the floor!
The thoughts gushing
try to make me run on my toes,
seek refuge in the dark,
beg the comfort of slumber
But sleep eludes me,
counting stars won't do the trick
So, I sit by my window
look over the empty streets,
blow smoke that crowns me
with yet another wave
of relentless musings
When will this torture end?
When will my mind rest?
For right now I want to escape
before the life in me hushes

-messy place

I wish you were
A Ken doll
I can play with
when I please,
strike hard when I'm pissed,
stock at the basement
when I don't need
you, but baby,
the heart that I wear shrieks
secrets I wish to keep
for myself
as the truth
slaps me hard
shaking me off my reverie
You are not a Ken doll
but a man—
a man I desire
And I?
I am the paper doll
you made in your spare time,
played with in your boredom
then you tore me apart,
ignoring my cries of pain,
ignoring my stunned face
Oh, you tossed me into the trash
Now I'm burning with the toys
you have grown weary of

-paper doll

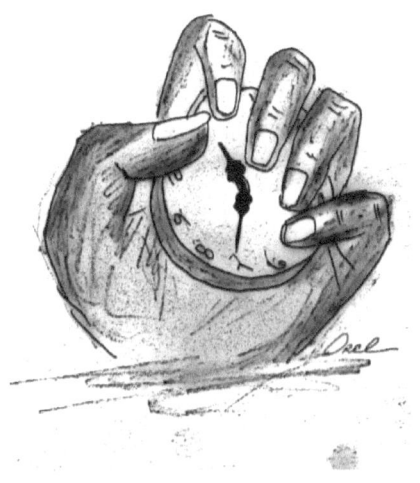

If I can manipulate time,
create a loop where I can hide
from the world, I will freeze
that moment we spent
writing poetry on napkins
preserve the bliss
preserve the *"you"* in it
so, I won't feel this devastated
with the thought of you leaving
me alone in this
one-way street

-*create a loop*

Sometimes
we end up
forgiving
people who don't
even recognize
their crimes

-forgiving

But what have become of us
after a lifetime of knowing?
It's hard to picture
how our hands used to fit,
how your fingers reach
to caress my face, the love
has long been buried
in time, I search
for the flame
as I try to keep
myself sane
What have become
of the words,
of the dream
we built?
Everything diminished
into ashes
Even the tear brimming
in my eyes dried up
in my lashes
before I could catch it

-what have become of us?

There are times
when saying *"I love you."*
pains me like
it was supposed to.

Gnashing teeth of betrayal
sank against my skin,
scarring me for eternity
So, when I strip
naked I reminisce
the way I was mishandled,
the lies spilled
all over the carpet, staining
the floor beneath
Every time I try
to fall in love, I die,
worried sick thinking
of another possibility
I could fall victim
to a wave of deceit

-how I was mishandled

Love asks for nothing
but surrender
You can't love
without opening up
until your heart
is in full view,
his for the taking
and you bleed
words you never knew
were stored deep within you
You're cracked open,
welcome the pain
Surrendering is
an arduous process
that forces
you to your knees
It's worth it
Trust the agony
It's a portal
to a world floating
on an asthenosphere
of milk and honey!

-surrender

Great things take time, they say
So, I'm waiting,
waiting, waiting...
Nothing's happening
Even the stars
that used to burn,
they hide tonight
I can't make them out
The blackness around me
makes it impossible to see things
But I'm waiting,
waiting for you
as I still believe
you're the greatest thing
that ever happened to me
despite the lies,
the shower of kisses
that almost took away
my life
I'm waiting darling
but there's no sign
of you walking into
that door again
Even a faint possibility
that you're coming back
as you promised you would
burns with the embers,
rises with the smoke
I still refuse to move
I positioned myself here
in this spot

so, I can see you from afar—
the greatness that you are
running towards me
with open arms
But *why, oh why?*
I've been here for a while
yet still, nothing's happening
I guess they're right
great things take time
for it did take time
for my faith to die
with everything else
My hope withers away
with my shattering heart

Great things take time
Yes, it did take time
for me to die!

-great things take time

I stopped writing,
stopped trying
to transform my pains
into words
screaming, deceiving
I stopped freeing
the voices in my head
taking over the pen
scribbling tons of mess
on papers then call it
art afterwards
while all I can see
are letters dancing
before my eyes
I stopped staining
blood against the wall
no matter how red
it appears, it won't
give justice to the life
I endure—
so much tragedy in a day!
I'm a thread stretched fiercely
I struggle not to break,
struggle not to write
or create
another piece that will grace
the half-filled trash bin
waiting, silently anticipating
at the corner

**-*trash bin waiting*

How am I supposed to leave
when a part of me clings
in your lips,
vehemently refusing
to detach as you sing
melodies,
that remind
me of the fire
that consumed the entirety
of my being
Those were the times
my darling,
when the universe
was kind,
and I was allowed
to call you mine!

-when the universe was kind

I left my heart open,
waiting for you
Exposed to the elements,
it beats weakly,
anticipating your return
But you've been gone
for epochs
my heart consumed itself
with its wrath,
drowned itself in blood
I am left with nothing
but an empty chest
as the love
I felt for you
became volatile,
it evaporated as swift
as a propanone

-propanone

All the dark parts
of my mind,
have you tried
to explore them?
They exude
colors too
Such vivid hues
depicting the aesthetic
that is me and you

-exude colors

You
who were so terrified
of my storm,
don't come
under my blue sky

You're not welcome
to join me there
anymore!

-under my blue sky

And you remained
to be
the ***ghost***
I keep summoning,
wishing
you will
appear
before my bed
and remind me
how it feels
to be alive!

But sadly,
as we age,
our hearts
***harden
into a stone***

How could you see
through my burning flesh
with those cold eyes,
unmoving like they're dead?
Though they twinkle,
enthrall me from time to time,
they glisten without a hint
of the outspoken mirth
You want me to believe
the lies I don't need
Come closer to my heart,
let your resolves shrivel
I may be a little confused
but I'll love you forever

-unmoving eyes

Like the snow
and the raindrop,
my heart does
what it does best:
it falls!

Listen,
for once
to my breaking heart
I wrote
a poem for you
but I tossed
it to the fire,
watched it burn
with my wrath
because the truth is
you don't even care

-wrote a poem for you

Death has an aesthetic sense
of calming my tensed nerves
He dropped by last night
to check if I'm alright
We chatted about demons
and how they cast torment
I told him about my darkness
he commented on my coldness,
chided me for being clueless
of how life is making me blessed
He lingered for coffee
as I talked about artistry
The night was getting dizzy
my eyes were getting heavy
but death stayed with me
like a loyal friend
and when the time comes
he left me undisturbed

-left undisturbed

Dark eyes staring
from the veil of numbness
blinding them from
the real world
Oh, they try to see
breaking the barrier
between the seven seas
where my swirling thoughts
and emotions are bottled,
ready to be swept away
to faraway shores
Wish I could smuggle
the truth away from here
for ears are deaf,
eyes are veiled
But yours—dark and deep
like an unknowable lake,
they stare,
revealing such passion
burning with all the things
I run away from:
love, fiery devotion—
all I deemed illusion,
unreal,
they stare back at me
through your eyes
as they sweep my face
in a sweet, tantalizing gaze

-unreal

I didn't die right there.

Or perhaps, *I did*. But the skin covering me waited for hundred million sunsets before totally collapsing, exposing the truth as to why my ghost chose to loiter here after death: *YOU!*

I got me into thinking
that our story
will have a beautiful ending.

Why did you have
to ***spoil everything
by leaving?***

I am peaceful now
as though the swirling storms
within me had passed
Now I am calm,
left with my clarity,
freed from those things
that confused me,
I am no longer mad
I have tamed my demons
like you taught me
I stand over the edge
of this dangerous cliff,
the city wakes,
the sun fights its way
through the shadows
The city rises,
I feel renewed
The old me is dead
Somehow this thought
consoles me more
than the arms
wrapped around my waist
Darling, you seem distant
Are you even real?
Are you even here—
watching the city wakes
with me?

-city wakes with me

The time is wrong
You
Me
This feeling
It's all wrong
Even the song
sounds like
it ***doesn't belong
to this century***

"I don't want to give the pains back." she agonized.
"*But you know how people can be ruthless!*"

I grew wings,
metamorphosed—
a pupa dreaming
to reach the sky
But as I begin to fly
your words
thwarted me
Like daggers
they maimed
my pride
I fell to the ground
hugging my knees, grieving—
for all the broken dreams
I could have held
if I did not
listen
to your thunderous
screams

-incomplete revolution

The singer sings
in bittersweet tune
Melancholy fills
his guitar strings,
fingers strum
gently yet fiercely
I am caught
in the middle
of the story his lips speak
Lost in translation, I swim
into the depth
of emotions spilling
through his words,
ripples of unrehearsed
thoughts sprinkling
droplets of tears
marking my cheeks,
tumbling down my handkerchief
He stopped strumming
suddenly searched my face,
eyes, a pair of roving lights
seeking for a shimmer of truth
he wishes to find
in my broken lies

-lost in translation

Long lashes sweeping
against your face,
such beauty veiling
eyes sparkling
with unspoken tales—
an ancient riddle
shrouding your soul
Darling you are the mystery
twisting my brain,
urging me to explore the truth
about the raging oceans,
hoping to meet you there
at the bottom, wandering
waiting for someone dauntless
to love you in your brokenness

-love you in your brokenness

I almost got it, you know
How your fingers curled
around mine
and that one swift glimpse
that sent me to cloud nine
collecting scattered wishes
we whispered to the stars
but were never granted
I remember how we leaned
against each other
comfortably wrapped in silence,
our hearts beating fast
Oh, my love I almost understood
but I missed the salient points—
how you broke in my embrace
not that it was too tight
but because it was too loose
to hold your breaking bones,
keep your pieces intact
You fell apart in my grasp
Now I am left wondering
as you chose to stow away
with the tears I bottled
to the other side of the ocean
I almost got it
I almost did
We almost made it
Now I weep, weep as I think
of how ***close*** we were
in convincing dear destiny

If the reason
you came back
is to rub salt
against my wounds,
darling, you don't get
the pass
to come in and out
of my heart
as though time
holds the damn door
open wide
for you!

-rub salt

I can't believe you kissed me
under the umbrella tree
one dreary afternoon
while I was writing our song
You pulled me close
oh, my mystic phantom!
Took my hand like you own
every screaming fiber in my body
You leaned to touch
my trembling lips,
I resisted at first,
yet overwhelmed by my thirst,
I drank all of you in
as though my life depended
on this tormenting kiss
I clung to your shoulder,
prayed it would last forever
But nothing lasts forever
You let go all of a sudden,
my face turned ashen
for when I looked up
I was staring at a face
of a total stranger

-*nothing lasts forever*

On the first draft,
the writer loved the muse
In the process of editing
she realized
love is not really
what she makes it
On the final draft
the writer killed the muse

-first and final draft

"Don't get attached child.",
advised the sage.
*"Notice how a litmus paper
turns red in acidic solutions.
That's how swift
your **value deteriorates**
when people
don't need you
anymore!"*

I have always harmed myself hoping to forget; hoping to convert my emotions into something physical and more bearable. Razor blades, pins and a punch on the wall, crazy as it sounds, *they became the proof that I do not merely exist. I am alive.* The gushing blood saved me from becoming totally numb. I've grown tired of it, nonetheless. I've grown used to the pain.

Now I found a new kind of self-harm: *loving you* even if you won't love me back. This is even more compelling; even more painful than inflicting a physical wound. Excruciatingly addictive, I can't stop myself from doing it. For it doesn't only tell me I am living. It reminds me of what I am capable of: LOVE.

So, I promise to do it every day. I'll make love to your memory every day, before they fade away like you did. I hope that in the end, this wishful thinking could kill me the way those wounds I tattooed all over my skin should have done a long time ago.

-make love to your memory

There was a time when roses bloom
We lay on a hammock,
watched the seagulls fly
as though waving goodbye
to the azure ocean
The waves crashed
against the patient shore
Our minds wandered
to different dimensions
We dreamed too much, *you and I*
Thought time was infinite
and poems are as ample
as the sand on the beach
Those were the times
and I remember them now,
realize how life
made us fall to its follies,
trapped us to find
a truth that is more elusive
than the dreams we sketched
on that wishful summer
Too many seasons gone by,
yet we still don't know what maims us most
Is it the knowledge that everything
will eventually turn into a memory
or this moment
when we find ourselves reminiscing
what we used to be?

-*memories*

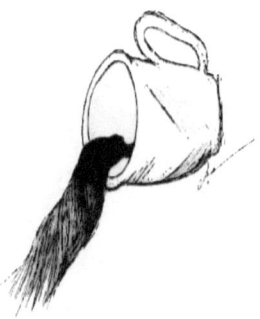

Love is like a coffee,
bittersweet and strong
but tastes good
all the time
A little cup of miracle—
like love, it gets cold
when it sits unnoticed,
its coldness sticks
on the lips,
a ghost haunting
a broken heart
causing it to shake,
as it falls into the pangs
But coffee can be reheated,
can be made sweet again
like the wound in your heart,
you can always mend it,
heal it
so, it can keep you alive
to survive
the longest night
So, pour me a cup
of that bittersweet miracle,
pour an ample of it
so, I can warm myself
in the midst
of the cruelest winter

-bittersweet miracle

Death
Slow death
Painful death
Sudden death
Black death
Death
All of which
had a fair chance
in trying
to zap my heart
but ended up
crawling back
to the void
where I now
reside
with my battle weary
soul
Death
Slow death
Painful death
Sudden death
Black death
Death
If you have come
again to take me home
at least pour
this cup
with my bottled sorrow
and I hope
we can chat
before we embark

to our journey
for I heard
no one talks
about
death
slow death,
painful death,
sudden death,
black death,
death
in paradise…

-death in paradise

I look about the room with my bloodshot eyes
Try to repress a shudder as dark shadows rise
I shriek out in anguish my depressing plight
Hope you would hear me out as my feelings ignite

Two AM—it is dark and cold
Wish I could see through you the secrets you hold
Two AM—my thoughts of you all brawled
Silently, I crumble; oh, my scorned soul—behold!

Still, I yearn to LOVE you, why can't you see?
Oh, hear I profoundly ask you, why can't it be?
Opened my heart for you, I bleed eternally
Still, I yearn to touch you, oh come to me

Two AM—my pained head keeps spinning
I am dizzy yet I struggle ferociously
Two AM—it never stopped raining
Drenched; I shiver against the cold enveloping me

I hope you would call for me when you're hurt
When frightened I wish you would seek me first
Cause for you I'm willing to slay dragons
I would burn, bleed, and swallow deathly poison!

But it's two AM and you're not seeing me
The walls are closing in; why won't you come to me?
It's two AM and still you're not here with me
My world starts to shatter—*redeem me!*

-two am

I was never
a halcyon sea
but you calmed my waves
with songs
I've never heard before

-halcyon

Let me get this straight, my darling. It's either you're in love with me or you're not in love with me. There's no middle ground. So, if you're not certain about how you feel about me, you can go. I've watched lovers walked out of that door so many times that I got used to seeing people leave. It will hurt a little but I definitely prefer being alone over spending time with someone who isn't sure about me.

Let me get this straight, my darling. ***I refuse to be half-loved.***

I've tried to catch love
but its shadows eloped
with ghosts of the past
I've called it
like I know its name,
tried to bottle it
as it falls with the rain
But didn't win it
so, I crumbled with my pain
Tried to bury it
with the pages it stained
Then the wind blows it
moments after I stopped searching,
its scent fills me
as it tickles my brain
My heart can't believe it
for its such an irony
that I found you
my love,
when I wasn't even looking

-found love when I wasn't even looking

The taste of your lips
lingered for a while
You kissed me goodnight,
drove me wanton and wild
Then ripples of silence
held me in their claws,
urging me to open
these eyes that I've closed
So, I opened them
saw you for the first time
felt the coldness in your breath
forced the dagger in your chest
then I sped away
like a bullet train
escaping the teeth
of infuriated justice

-infuriated justice

Baby don't cy
for I'll let you slip
through my fingers
like a running stream
Regardless of how they beat,
we can never own our hearts
Let them wander through time,
sing their own rhyme,
listen to their faint stirrings
resound across century—
a love carved through eons
crying out in liberty
Baby just let it be
your heart will one day
in my solitude, find me
For what the universe
has put together
will find their place
like pieces that complete
a gargantuan puzzle
Soulmates will find each other
in the most opportune time

-soulmates

Walking around town, a lot of things fascinate me. Like how the streets seem to be unemptied, how gently the droplets of rain kiss the cobblestones, how strangers communicate so much with a nod, or a smile, or a wave of a hand. As I immerse my melancholic self into the heart of the bustling metropolis, my eyes are glued to a boy kneeling before a girl, tying her shoelaces. I am not particularly enthralled by the picturesque image of him tying her shoelaces. I wonder if people were shoelaces that could lose their grips on reality once in a while, how many are willing to be there, help tie them up so they won't eventually lose their souls into oblivion.

-shoelaces

The space you occupied a moment ago, someone sat there. I wonder if he could feel your warmth from the wooden chair, or smell your scent from the chilled air. From where I am seated, I could feel the life escaping from you, baby. The faint stirrings from your barely beating heart become the shattering sound that fills my ears. I wish I had told you what you meant while you were still here.

Now it's too late…*too late for confessions!*

-*felt you from the wooden chair*

How do we break gently, when the force is an avalanche dragging us upside down? Can we allow ourselves the luxury of time to scream? Are we supposed to swallow the fear rising up with the storm inside us?

Sometimes we're doomed to hurt in silence. For when we say a word, no one will listen. If somebody listens, they hardly understand. The hands that we grab when the pain is too much are just fingers curling around ours—ropes gripping tightly but don't give off warmth. Still, we freeze to death. What do we do? We deny the pain, try to pretend to be someone we're not, yet again.

-*someone we're not*

I wish
when you learn
to stare
at life,
it will blink
back at you
and you will
believe
it's not cold
or empty
Life feels
you as you feel
it shatters
under your feet
sometimes…

-life

If you get a chance
to break my skull,
find out
that my head contains
a chaotic sky,
will you still stay?
Or you will remain
to be the happiness
I run on my toes
Elusive
as the unmade
memories swirling
over my grave

-my head contains

You promised
to meet me "there"
but you never showed up
I sat on a rock,
watch the colors fade
to grey
Stiff, immobile,
I am alive
yet my heart sounded
like a dead clock
screaming out
"there" is an illusion
and I have been deceived
There is no "there"
neither is there a "you"
or an "us"

-"there" is an illusion

There will be pain
along the way
This may even bury you beneath
wounded skin,
fill you with angst
and melancholic hymns
and all those things
you we're protected from
In those moments I hope
you'll remember what I told you
about how your roar
can scare all the demons
back to the grave

-beneath wounded skin

We don't love them
when they're here
sitting next to us,
breathing in
words we spit
We don't even
look at them
or listen
when they talk
We simply don't care
until the hands
that used to warm
us have become
corpses
haunting
our every dream

-love them here

I want to talk about what goes inside my head. However, I don't know how or where to begin. Shall I say something about the old *azotea* first? Or it would be more appropriate to describe the garlands you tied around my head, petals scattering beneath our feet as we swirled about in a frantic dance. I never thought it would be this difficult to describe that moment time has diminished into a vivid memory that won't leave my mind. Your face still enthralls me that sometimes I find myself smiling. It's insane. You're gone but the flowers we picked are still inside the pocket of my jeans, each dried petal reminds me of how they smelled—of how you smelled under the glow of the sun, sweat dripping from your hair to the tip of your nose.

-frantic dance

Soothing Ironies

You came up to me, a rather tenacious whiplash
Chained me, confined me, dragged me to my doom
Beat me, skinned me, burned me to ashes
My remains you scattered; my bones about the room

You dragged me six feet underground
Hear me as I bellow my call
You dragged me six feet underground
 You left me with nothing at all

I smoked all your threats, drank ounces of your lies
I swallowed false salvation, watched you roll the dice
Made me a bed of pythons, heard you laughed while I shrieked
Proclaimed you are my savior, how blinded I had been

You drank my blood till I fell so frail
From the valley of my death, you hail
You put me six feet underground, so dark I couldn't see
My bones shattered to pieces; oh, how cruel my love can be!

I'm underground, so chilled I need some warmth
To touch my soul, set my spirit free
Lift the veil blinding me, I need to see
Free me from the verge of your hell-bound wrath!

My darling you grumbled like a mad dog!
Thought you loved me; it seems you never could
For you dug my grave like a nemesis would
How frosty you look from where you stood!

-underground

We shared a love
yet ended up
revising the plot
making each other
the antagonists
of the whole
romantic craft.

-antagonists

The world keeps spinning,
spinning against me
The hand of the clock points
to where I stand drenched
in my salty sweat,
I look like a disaster
in the making,
thoughts swirling
about the empty room,
driving me to the edge
of desolation
I long for a drink
at two in the afternoon
Perhaps the alcohol could wash
all the pain draining my guts
Or perhaps I need a little morphine
to numb me from within
so, I can stop screaming
The walls are deaf
but I tried wailing,
beseeching the gods
to stop me from shaking
But as I reach for the sturdy
wall, the world collapses
and I crumble with it,
my voice swallowed
by the crowd
cheering beneath
my feet

-disaster in the making

The past isn't *chasing* me but I *run*—run from the shadows, the disembodied voices, the faces forming on the wall, on the ceiling, on the cumulus clouds. I run from the ruins, the curtains waltzing with the morning breeze, the embers licking the wood, the clock that stopped functioning. All of these things are dead ringers of the you I used to know. Though you don't haunt me like you vowed you would, the emptiness in my chest does.

Darling, you went away so quietly. I wish I could have known. Our memories don't chase me like you promised they would but I run away from them nonetheless. And why should I not? My bath soap smells like you that I can't indulge in a foamy lather without the vision of your skin teasing my mind. The toast I made this morning echoes the hazy breakfast conversations I've had with you. My car keys, the traffic lights, the cologne worn by the person who stood next to me at the bus stop...*everything*. I run away darling, speed with the wind to an unknown destination. I run away wishing, you will come after me.

-dead ringers

You look down at me with those warm, gentle eyes
Can't feel anything, my heart's a dark steely ice
My lips speak of nothing but stark, ghastly lies
For I'm a dark soul ***cast from the skies***

Yet I could feel my blood flowing when you're near
It's as though I am alive for one more while
I could hear my heart throbbing when you are here
Your voice gives me courage to walk one more mile

I try to reach you as I draw closer to the dark
Try to feel your warmth as my soul desolates from sin
I shout out your name; I long to see your light spark
Come run to me before Gehenna swallow me in

My feet stumble as I walk this thorny path
My courage so frail that it crumbles with my wrath
I glimpse back at you yet I could hardly make you out
Need to see you once more before death swirls me about

I wish I could fall freely in your arms before my demons creep
And perhaps you would catch and hold me closely as I weep
I long so much for solace, a heavenly dream in my sleep
Since I vanished from paradise, these comely thoughts I keep

With my outstretched arms I spin as my blood gushes out like stream
In this labyrinth I loiter, in the pangs of exile I revel
And still, I flinch with each blow; with each callous whip I scream
I wish you could lift me up—save me from this anguish forever!

But when we kiss
you hiss
Oh, I drink you in,
oblivious of
the venom
sprouting
from your lips

-oblivious

How do we forgive
the eyes that saw
beyond visage
the moonlight has touched,
unraveling buried
secrets beneath
stone cold flesh
How do we forgive
the lips that mumbled
words so kind, at last
the fortress crushed
exposing the soul
we tried so hard to protect
from the corroding world
How do we forgive
the fingers that traced
our nape as we were waking,
gentle as a dew gliding
against the window glass,
the emotions they evoked
matched the fury
of the storm rising
beyond the horizon
How do we forgive
darling, the misty apparition
the things we have come to believe,
the words we learned to speak,
the ticking of the clock—
echoes of the time we've lost,
the withered flowers
the empty chocolate boxes

the songs with empty lyrics
How do we forgive
the love we luckily grasped
but was ***never meant to last?***

There's a part of me
that lingers
on the walls,
in the sheets
and it
holds you still
loves you still—
a part no one can steal,
a void no one can fill!
For even in your absence
you occupy it
Your weight
makes me feel so empty
I guess I am cursed
to feel a love
I cannot own,
endure the longing
that lasts
even after the day
you left me heartbroken
My world crumbled
with the waves
shrieking out your name
I stayed true
to my promise
to cherish your memory
like I own you
Stayed true to it
when you decided to go
and I was bereft of reasons
All the days after that

my love, I've been crawling
beneath the sheets, watching
you fall asleep
from behind the walls
My tears are the only
company that I keep
as I vow to the wind
to trace the steps
that we walked
praying to catch a glimpse
of where I fell short
and make it up to you

-part that lingers

Now you turned
into the sad
poem
that I wrote
under the glow
of the moon,
sulking with the shadows,
dancing with the trees
while I hum
Oh, you turned
into the sad
song
that you sang
under the glow
of the sun
crumbling with the waves,
sweeping against the shore
while you run
while I hum
Oh, we run
while we hum
and I wrote
and you sang
a sad poem
a sad song—
melancholy
dripping,
colliding
with the sound
vibrating
Oh, you sang

oh, I wrote
Yeah, we rhymed
then we drifted
as you ran
Then I began
to rewrite
the ending

-sad poem

If you look back far enough, you can see....

tears stained on stars,
hearts contained in penny jars,
words queued on my tongue
trying to roll themselves out
Also, there are blisters on the moon
a laceration on its side, scribbles of who we are
decorating the path where I stride

Helpless yet devoted
to the corpse that you are,
mindless of the pouring
of the gust whispering *"He is gone!"*
It's time to move forward
but my eyes keep looking backward
to where we have talked
our last few sentences,
such a painful farewell
I am trying to get by

If you looked back far enough,
you would have seen me crawl,
pick my pieces scattered
all over the floor
But you stared far ahead
cold, uncaring heart
turning into a memory, a scar taking niche
into the skin that I wear

-blisters on the moon

And she learned
to sleep ***through the pain***
for the night
won't make it go away

I crawl under the blanket,
hide from the world
for it lied in my face
told me it won't hurt
But I crumbled then and there,
a figurine breaking
into thousand pieces
diminishing
into thousand wishes
foolishly cast
to the galaxies
A time wasted,
darling I am
a butterfly enslaved
within the chambers
of your devouring heart

-figurine breaking

It's midnight,
you hold me
for the shortest time,
plant kisses—
small marks of blindness
along my spine
I smile,
pull you closer
like you're mine
and not loaned
to me by the tides
Incandescent lights
play with my eyes
You're pulling away
from me
Cut the thread
that connects you to me
as the sheets
begin to feel
like Pleistocene
But your heart urges me
to commit a sin,
and I would sin
as you lean
for the shortest time,
breathe you in
in an anguished sigh
before you disappear
with the grey sky

-marks of blindness

Poems—
they say these
ought to evoke
emotions one must feel
Every beat
of the poet's heart
manifesting in every line,
even those
which are lost
in the rhymes
must be felt,
tasted with the tears
held up for years
So, I write
hoping to ink
the *you* I wish
to remember,
the *you* I wish
to linger
but left
nonetheless

-poet's heart

May my tears wash away
the imprints you made
in my heart,
your claw marks
all over my skin—
a history etched,
painfully destined
to have an audacious comeback
through **_him_**
He cradles my withering body,
catches my labored breath
in his palms,
in his lips
pretending,
always pretending
to measure
the depth
of my sorrow,
a Baikal
of hidden cravings
running with
my salty tears

-*baikal of cravings*

If someday,
Fate betrays
me and you change,
your heart turns
into a chilled steel
that doesn't feel
a beat
for me,
I hope you will
lie—
say that you love me,
swear that you need me

If one day
the tides will begin
to turn against me
and you feel
like you can no longer stay
I hope you will
lie—
promise you won't leave me
though your heart
is already halfway
there

-chilled steel

The ink stained
along the pages
remains
a reminiscence
of *what we were*—
hearts sprinkled
in a story
we never wish
to live
while we exist
miles apart
from where
we felt the spark
Our prints are gone,
the heartbeats linger
with the clumsy promises
of forever!

-saudade

Pliant

I try to be pliant
but may I speak,
empty the *void*
I carry
May I speak
for a minute
I won't need
much time to grieve
I try to be pliant
though I break
in the process, I try
wishing I would win
the war raging
But the thing
about the soothsayers,
sometimes they veil
the truth with anything
They said love always wins
so, I bent
waiting for the kiss of spring
It never came
Seasons passed, it never came
All my tears turned to dust
The soothsayers veiled
the truth that *love doesn't always win*
For when it is,
then you would be here
recounting your day with me

-*soothsayers*

The sun set quietly in the west,
Shadow of death lurked over his bed.
Darkness has crept now it was night,
Poor Anton Blue reached for the light.

All alone and yet he felt calm.
Mem'ries came, in his head they swarmed.
Salad days he knew now were gone.
Gone to the west, set with the sun.

Anton couldn't clearly make out.
What he did with the life he once had?
When hope threatened to break up,
What became of the courage he had?

The years had grown cruelly cold.
His hair turned grey, now he was old.
He searched in his heart the creed he once told,
The dream he kept when still he was bold.

But of course, they were gone, set with the sun.
Now night loomed, darkness ate in his soul.
Anton turned; *there was no one to call.*
His time was up, it ran out with the sand.

In his deathbed he wished somehow, he could dream.
In the verge of anguish, he wished he could scream,
Just how much he regrets the time he had wasted.
If only *he'd lived*, then *life he could have tasted!*

But now all is through with poor Anton Blue.
He watched the light burned in its brilliant glow.
For once he begged death to come on slow.
Soon he succumbed, it's due, poor Anton Blue!

-anton blue

Wandering in the clouds
then back to your eyes
where I feel
more fulfilled,
sanity intact
In my dream
my lips rake
the softness
of your skin,
breath moves
through the air
that surrounds us
syncing with the storm
of thoughts
fading with the colors
Now the room
is painted black,
our eyes locked
for a fleeting hour,
one fleeting hour!

Then you're gone
Then you're gone…

-nubivagant

Ana Grasya

Slumped on the floor, I soliloquize
Oh, *to be or not to be*
Hush, my mind!
be *still...*
Be still, little heart,
you're drumming loud
again, I can't hear
the whispers,
you're drowning
the call
To be....
I want to be
near the hills,
where he promised
his heart to me
To be...
or not to be
distracted from his
warm stares again,
Hush, my mind!
You're debating
with me again!
He's the broken
fragment of a glass
I saw scattered
Fixed him with my hand
so, he can be....
so, he'd be...
whole?
But it is I who *crumbled!*
Be still, little heart,

Cling to your clarity
We can't be
holding a piece
that won't complete the puzzle
Hush, my mind!
We can't be yearning
for a touch
that won't smooth
out the creases
To be…
or not to be…
We can't run after
the one who doesn't
want to stay
We can't expect
the one who broke us
to turn back
and care
Be still, little heart
stop *waiting…*
For healing won't come
from the hand—
from the very hand
that forced
the poison into our mouth!

-soliloquize

My lipstick stained
your white shirt,
a *scintilla*
of an ephemeral love—
a brief kiss
at my porch
as the moon beamed,
stars twinkled
with knowledge
of the erratic heartbeat,
fingers entwined,
eyes dazed,
words resounding
promises we won't keep
The wind knew
Now I wonder
if it tried to warn me
as it blew my hair
the moment
you disappeared
into the dark alley

-scintilla

May your jeans
remember
my hands
tucked into its pocket,
an abditory I need
when the world gets loud
and the rain won't stop
pouring,
drowning
me into an ocean
of emptiness
May you feel
baby, the weight
of my absence
before
you bury my scent
deep into oblivescence!

-abditory

We don't heal
by avoiding
the wounds
or escaping
the gunshots
We don't heal
by speeding past
the knives,
preventing scars
from forming
We heal
by breaking,
by cutting
our hearts
into pieces
We become whole
by cicatrizing first!

-cicatrize

The room closes in,
walls becoming
whiter, emptier,
curtains swaying
intensifying
the truth
that I am alone again
drowning in my tears
losing it in my screams
I fall silent,
reach for the phone,
dial a number
I've memorized
for so long
The voice
from the other line
breaks with mine
I end the call, realizing
in this time
of loneliness
nothing can fill
the void gaping
but myself

-fill the void gaping

Why is it that when I read poems,
I feel you between the lines,
see you through the imagery,
hear you throb with the rhymes?
Could it be that the poets
have known you better
than I do
that they were
able to capture you
into their words
while I trip and fall
chasing the heart
that you stole

-my love in other people's poems

When will you realize
that the tears falling
from your eyes
are proof
of a strength
crawling in your skin
The shuddering
of your flesh
is a trace of the bravery
you let loose
The wavering
of your voice
resounds the battle cry
you roared
so, all of the passersby
halted to listen
When will you realize
that your unpolished sides
are token
from the wars you've won
You may be broken
darling
but you are not fragile!

-broken but not fragile

If I could speak
to the heart
that is now dead
I would ask it
if it's colder
there, in the grave
If it tells me, yes
then I will stay here
with you
where your arms
wrap me
into a chilly embrace

-wrap into chilly embrace

I have to stand when standing's not easy
For when it is what joy is there to feel?
I need to have faith when the tide is against me
Who knows one day it'll succumb to my will?

My eyes have seen how the waves cruelly tumbled
In this world the weak's always the first to crumble
You would not live long if you are not capable
Of picking yourself up each time you stumble

The path to success is never plain
It is never lenient; never tame
It's rather dreary, truculent and rough
Those who could tread it are the brave and tough

And so, I've sworn not to quit when I fall
To bend, to roll but never to crumble
To shudder, to bleed but never surrender
I'd fight till I win, a determined soldier

Even the wind tries to blow me down
I get up patiently, a knight so gallant
Even the storm tries to smash me down
I struggle fearlessly, a heart so valiant

I will always stand when standing is not easy
I will walk straight and sturdy as can be
I will not give up when the tide's against me
Soon it will bow and succumb to me in my victory!

-when standing is not easy

But when I stopped
beseeching the gods,
gave up summoning
the past,
I spotted you
from my window glass
arms outstretched—
calling me out
I unbolted the door,
froze at your presence,
chided Fate
for the irony
of you
coming back to me
the moment I stopped
wanting you

-summoning the past

I let you into
my heart,
which, at the moment
was hurting
from a bitter past
I learned to crawl
to wholeness,
healed as fast as I could
to attend to your wounds,
stop them from bleeding
Sealed your lips with mine,
gave my life
to stellify
your eyes
Apparently,
you held a dagger
in your hands,
thrusted it deep
into my flesh
then sped
away, leaving
me pondering
on the words of Aristotle
"Sense of tragedy
comes ironically
not from the protagonist's
weak points
but from his
good qualities!"

-stellify your eyes

Of all the masks
you wear,
you have
always been transparent
The real *you* bask
into the warmth
of the psychedelic lights
roving
I see you
Your truth, darling
is exuded,
eclipsing the visage
No more hiding,
come out,
set *you* free
My arms are waiting
Let the facade
shrivel until it falls
Beam with the truth
you tried to conceal
deep within…

-transparent

She isn't your answered prayer.
She nags.

She isn't your answered prayer.
She argues.
She questions your intention.

She isn't your answered prayer.
She bleeds.
She crumbles.
She isn't perfect.

She isn't your answered prayer.
Sometimes she crawls back to her hide.

She isn't your answered prayer.
She lets negative thoughts swarm inside her head.
She drains the energy out of you.

She isn't your answered prayer.
She doubts.
She curses.
She remembers her traumas.

She isn't your answered prayer.
She drives you to the wall.

She isn't your answered prayer.
She shatters the illusion of a perfect relationship.
She isn't the ideal girl.

She isn't your answered prayer.
But she chose you over others who pursued her.
She tries to silence her demons when you're near.
She compromises.

She isn't your answered prayer.

But same
you
should the
love just
her

-*answered prayer*

Why do we
tend to feel
complete
the moment
we give
away ***a piece
of our heart?***

I looked at the sky,
saw you twinkled
in mirth
Seemingly too
close yet
too distant, I
rehearsed
countless speeches
I could say to you
to make you fall,
make you mine
None registered
The words waltzed
their way
out of my brain

I stood there,
Made a deal with Fate
If he could turn
you into a shooting star
I'll cast a wish

- *too close yet too distant*

I have written countless poems
about you
and you have sung countless songs
about me
but the idea of *us*
escapes our fingertips
Maybe there is something
about love
that could not be
captured,
could not be
put into words,
could not be
turned into a song
But that something
lingers, a magic
circling, binding
us darling
into one
ethereal being!

-idea of us

Thoughts could run as remote as the truth that governs human existence. I walk along the streets, a little intoxicated but incredibly conscious of the lingering stares from strangers. As my feet touch the ground, I could feel the earth shift for the first time in twenty-seven years, as though I was asleep for all those times and it was only at this very grave that my blood is flowing in frenzy—telling me I am *alive*. I try to clear my head so I could vividly make out everything that's unfolding before my eyes. It is such a heady feeling and I wanted to savor each passing emotion like I will never have a chance to feel this way again. I cross the street without bothering to cast a glimpse on the traffic lights, daring death, undaunted of the uncertainties of afterlife. I walk like I own my steps, my life, my destination. I'm heading home though I'm a little unsure if it's still the place I used to know: *warm and consoling*. And as I try to feel the vibration, the sound, the life revolving around me, I ask the gods why is it that I feel more austerely alive when I'm face to face with death?

-alive when faced with death

Love makes us feel young
and free
and excited
about today
and tomorrow
completely forgetting
all of yesterday's sorrow
Sweet as the nectar
of a freshly picked Santan,
we are milk and honey
engulfing each other, we
are free
to fly across the skyline
And if we ever fall,
we wish to bounce
like a ball
and ricochet our way
from the bludgeoning
storm rising
above the rivers
drawn by the hand
that crafted
our story into a poem

-ricochet our way

Some time in the past,
23:52

To you have I loved:

I wanted to run away—forget this crazy stuff and flee. Yet in the verge of my cynicism, something held me back and kept me waiting, gripped in the throes of desolation. This is not me—all these infernal longings that had me walking on threads. I know I've gone beyond *rational* in making the choice to endure the time that we have, though in spite of myself and all these intoxicating emotions swirling me about, I could feel it fleeting. I hope I could still have the courage to back out because this is wrong. Everything about this thing I've tried so hard to evade, is despairingly wrong.

I did not fail, I try to tell myself that. My resolves were firm enough to have kept me bold until the moment I've known you can destroy me. I might have recognized the frightful stirring—the deafening sound of my own heart breaking as it opened up for you. But I didn't mind. I refused to listen to the reverberating sound of my intellect screaming. I know I shouldn't fall. But despite my fierce rebuff, I fell like a giant feather—suspended in the air with my whole lungs bursting. For oft, I was greatly haunted by the thought that you might step back and let me fall to my doom as you see me gained significant speed. I can honestly profess the fear that had fed into my soul like a voracious vulture, draining me of the sanity I might have left. No matter how much I wanted to conceal it from you, a part of me never let me to. And so, I bared it completely so you could have a glimpse of me shattering.

It would be so silly to say this but I want you to know, I think this thing has to end now. I may have said it clearly enough that I do not believe in love and already lost faith in commitment but deep inside my frightened heart, *I do*. Those things I've told you about; all the cynicism has nothing to do with the naïve girl that I once was and still am. I needed walls to protect me for I am vulnerable. But now all those walls I erected are slowly crumbling, exposing the frightened girl in me. I don't want you to know this. I don't want anyone else to know this. But I do want you to have clarity—of what you think we have; of what this is. *This isn't real.* Though I could feel all my resolves wither away with your touch, there's no truth in everything that's going on between us. This may be strong enough to have had me consumed in day dream, but in the heart of these tenacious emotions confusing me, I know, with all certainty that what we have is the biggest hoax time could ever stage. Nothing but deceit—ruthless lies stabbing me right against my chest, causing me to die deaths I would never deserve.

Call me coward. Scream into my face that I'm so consumed with negativity. But let me tell you frankly, I'm doing this with the little courage I could muster. It's not that I don't want this. *Every fiber of my being shrieks out how much I needed this.* If there's such thing as salvation, it could be this—finally! I've been waiting. For the longest time, I've been longing for someone to come along, cast the darkness away, look into my eyes and tell me to stop shaking for nothing could hurt me now. But if salvation would mean breaking into pieces yet again, then let me just simply vanish. Let me just fall freely to my death and learn to live underground forever.

Yes, I wanted to run away. To rush back to my grave and hide away. I was fine living in the shadows. I dismissed all sorts of reminiscence; all stuff that could remind me *I was once alive.* I let the curtains fell, surrounded me with infinite darkness; shrouded me as I wept. I didn't think about how warm my flesh had been or how good the gentle rain had felt against my face. *Death had given me the solace I never imagined when I was alive.* I was fine living six feet underground—until you came. Without preamble, you came. I watched you thread the space between life and death with incredible valor, my very own Lochinvar in the flesh. With darkness slipping away from my grasp, I could feel my own blood running for the first time. It was easy to reclaim my humanity as I held your gaze for what seemed like infinity. And just like that, you had won me. In a split second though, it's over. In the end, you just became the *tenacious force pushing me back to my grave* where I've lain bleeding for the last one hundred years.

I wanted to run away. Now I wish, I did while I had the chance....

Forever drowned in irony,

Your past love

I walked so straight and sturdy that an aloof observer could immediately dismiss me as an accomplished young woman who knows where she's headed. No one would ever suspect from a glance that once, I decided to end my all with a razor blade. In spite of myself, I suddenly found it funny. I laughed and hastened my paces. Tomorrow, I am going to add another tattoo, the one I've wanted to imprint on my skin since high school. " *Audentis fortuna iuvat.*" (Fortune favors the brave.) It would seem *ironic* for in fact, I've never really been that brave. But here's the thing, *I've got reasons.*

Finally, I reached my car. Bittersweet thoughts crossed my mind as I unlocked it and sped past the busy street. Last year, he was here with me reading crazy anecdotes from the pile of Reader's Digest I compiled at the backseat. What was the last thing he told me before he went out of my door? *I love you, Ana?* Did he really? I doubled my speed as the glow of the afternoon sun started to fade out from my sight. He really told me that did he? But still *he left.* Why was that?

I made a turn as it started drizzling. The sky must be suffering my pains. I tripled my speed that I felt like flying recklessly. I thought of all the promises he made, the lies, the sweet nothings. I chose to believe his words, love his sins, accept his tormenting passion. And what did I get from choosing to hold him after all these years?

The road was getting slippery from the drizzles that I began to lose control. I tried to hit the break but could not seem to find it. I uttered a silent prayer as my hand shivered from panic. I was drenched in perspiration. Everything was moving so fast, I felt so confused and terrified. Then out of nowhere, another car approached without premonition. I shrieked. Yes, dear Lord, I confess I really decided to end it all with a razor blade, a noose, a deathly dose of coffee. But believe me, I don't want to die. Not now. Not yet.

Not ev—!

I felt the first stab of pain as I heard creaking everywhere. Blood oozed from my wounds—I was not sure how many wounds were bleeding at the moment. One thing was clear, it was excruciating. Then I felt cold. I gave a jerk and shivered. I looked around me, everything was black. Deafening sirens came from all directions, it seemed. Someone lifted me, I was lightweight. I closed my eyes though everybody told me not to fall asleep. But I did. And the last thing I remembered before I succumbed to the call of eternal slumber was coffee.

A black, freshly brewed coffee.

- *coffee break*

Silent
but loud
Halcyon
but squally
A fire raging wild
she soothes blisters and burns
Feeling safe
in the chaos,
she seeks refuge
from a storm
Lacerations
from her last fall
badly broken,
yet seems whole
Mind swirling,
thoughts cascading
Not a song
but bears a tone,
Not a poet
but writes poems
A nomad
seeking home!

-nomad

Why do these poets
bleed words whenever they talk?
Spill daggers wherever they walk,
shedding salty tears all over the sidewalk!
And the window pane
where they watched
the pouring rain
formed their image
from the fog
I envy them writing
word after word
that will eventually paint
the story
of my life, oh they grieve
over a stranger's broken heart
These poets,
they compose literature
from my angst,
breathe life to my muted
thoughts, now I sing
melancholy over the rainbow
These poets, they make me cry
as they try
to personify
all the rage boiling
inside my chaotic mind!

He—
does he give you second thoughts
about everything you've known?
Love
Time
Chances
Does he make your heart
clash
with your mind
while sending
powerful electricity
through your spine?
When you touch
does the world
suddenly stops?
Does he make you mad
then swallow
your pride?
Does he drive you crazy
thinking of him
in the middle of the night?
Does he make you want to flee
and at the same time
stay
in love with him?
Does he make you change your mind?
If he does, breathe him in,
all of him
Fill your lungs with his soothing ironies
Hold him
for nothing will ever look

more catastrophic
yet beautiful
than the one destined
to rearrange the chaos
in your head,
realign your path,
feed your heart
with tales
that will make it
repair its broken wings
and resurrect
the child—
the *innocent child* in you
who believes
in happy endings!

-soothing ironies

About the Author

Ana Grasya

Ana Grasya started writing at the age of 13 after being introduced to the legendary king Gilgamesh who ventured to seek for the secret of immortality but failed. Such failed conquest gave Ana an epiphany. What if this secret lies in a pen and a piece of paper? She has never stopped writing since.

Determined to improve her craft, Ana exposed herself to wide array of literary works in all of her high school years. In college, she became a staff of the CSU Communicator where she glimpsed the essence of writing for posterity. Now a licensed teacher, Ana realizes the paramount importance of representing people and their stories in literature. Establishing a niche in the field, she became fascinated with capturing the depth and intricacies of human emotions and experiences in poetry, hoping to touch a soul or two.

Her first book, Bygones was nominated for the Filipino Readers' Choice Award 2022.

www.ingramcontent.com/pod-product-compliance
Lightning Source LLC
LaVergne TN
LVHW091636070526
838199LV00044B/1093